FAREWELL, SUMMER

Also by Helen Hooven Santmyer

". . . And Ladies of the Club"

Ohio Town

Herbs and Apples

The Fierce Dispute

FAREWELL, SUMMER

Helen Hooven Santmyer

ILLUSTRATIONS BY DEBORAH HEALY

1817

HARPER & ROW, PUBLISHERS, New York
Cambridge, Philadelphia, San Francisco, Washington
London, Mexico City, São Paulo, Singapore, Sydney

 For information address Harper & Row, Publishers, Inc., 10 East 53rd Street, New York, N.Y. 10022. Published simultaneously in Canada by Fitzhenry & Whiteside Limited, Toronto.

FIRST EDITION

Copy editor: *Jean Touroff*

Designer: *Lydia Link*

Library of Congress Cataloging-in-Publication Data

Santmyer, Helen Hooven, 1895–
Farewell, summer.

I. Title.
PS3537.A775F37 1988 813'.52 87-45822
ISBN 0-06-015889-1

---

88 89 90 91 92 MPC 10 9 8 7 6 5 4 3 2 1

All a green willow, willow, willow,
All a green willow is my garland.

—JOHN HEYWOOD

FAREWELL, SUMMER

Chapter One

When I came back to Sunbury, toward the end of May, one of the first people I met uptown was Cousin Tune. I was walking on the courthouse side of the street, where the elms arch highest over the sidewalk, rising in a long perspective of one curve beyond another, and flowing down again in a leafy screen toward the grass in the square. The lowest twigs of the farthest tree brush back and forth across the Civil War cannon that stands in a corner of the lawn. From under that lovely green and golden vaulted ceiling I watched an old man crossing Main Street, and saw him stop at the curb for an instant like an unsteady child. When he drew abreast of the cannon, I recognized him. It was then that I was startled awake, by his age, to the relentless passage of the years.

Until this spring of 1935, I had been away for a long while, teaching or studying, writing more or less scholarly papers for whose material I had needed to live in the neighborhood of the great libraries here or abroad. If Cousin Tune had died in my absence I should probably not have heard about it, since there was no one to send me word; if I had thought, I should have supposed him dead long ago. But if I hadn't met him in the square that morning, I should not be writing this now; his being alive has made that difference to me.

For this isn't the book I intended to write, in solitude, in Sunbury's peace and quiet. It was a queer impulse that brought me back, with a suitcase full of notes and outlines. But now that I am settled, it seems wholly right that I should be here. When the world is sick of many ills, the place to be in is the place where you belong; you will find reassurance there, in a tall tree, in the grass, a flower—in the gentle contour of hills, pasture, and wood. "As water to our thirst, so is the rock, the ground, to our eyes and hands and feet." In Sunbury I had come as near that feeling as I ever came anywhere; the town had been home to my mother's people for many generations, and whenever my father, who was in the consular service, found himself stationed in a place unhealthy or unhandy for children, he sent me here to live with my grandparents.

I was brought back this spring by one of those uncanny clairvoyant flashes across the mind, one of those seconds that is recognized as unforgettable even as it passes. I had been in Oxford all winter, doing some unimportant research work into the life of a poet dead and gone centuries ago. One afternoon, circling the reading room of the Radcliffe Camera, intent on finding an empty space on one of the tables where I might put down my books, I came to an empty chair and stopped to pull it out. At once I was obscurely conscious of a threat, a menace, physical and actual, looming behind me. I turned and saw over my head the outstretched arm of Mercury, of the Winged Mercury, life-size, in plaster. Instantly, although I was there, I was also far away in time and place, back in school again, passing through a wide, dark hall under Mercury's caduceus, seeing again that lifted heel draped with a soiled handkerchief, or a bookstrap, or a lost cap. I was startled; my head was full of a cry: "What are *you* doing *here?*" It was as if I had been transported unchanged from that noisy, unaired hall, a child with untidy plaits, in a faded gingham dress and scuffed shoes, to this solemn place where anyone who looked at me could see I had no right to be. If anyone had looked, I should have felt the shame one suffers in dreams of being naked on the street. The instant passed; I tucked my chin into the furs at my throat and was reassured. Nevertheless I knew, then and for always, that the child Elizabeth Lane was I, still.

The Camera, the Bodleian, the path between them, the courtyard behind the Clarendon Building and the passage through it, where I had walked so carelessly, as if at home, now became strange to me, as though my presence were a betrayal of the child I had been. The feeling was wholly irrational, because the young Elizabeth Lane had lived in Sunbury dreaming of a future life in ancient, glamorous towns far away—irrational, and yet it brought me back.

I was sensible enough to finish the research I was doing; the results, the conclusions to be drawn, could be set down on paper anywhere. But so far I haven't touched that work, because of the conversation I had with Cousin Tune on the street that day.

I hadn't seen him for more than thirty years, but when he drew near I knew him. Or perhaps I knew the white linen suit, the walking stick, the panama hat with the wide brim. I felt as if there should be roller skates on my feet, and as if I were risking Grandmother's disapproval if I should stop to speak to him. But I had always stopped.

When we met he recognized me immediately, and

swept off his hat with the wide gesture that once upon a time had enabled me to see him in brocade coat, with lace at his wrists and a ruffled shirt. He bowed over my hand with the same elaborate courtesy he had exhibited when it was a child's grubby fist. I had always thought he was the politest man I knew, and I had loved him for it. But now the grace of his bow was marred by the stiffness of his bones, and he stood slope-shouldered, leaning on his stick. He smiled, and it was almost the old smile, slight, humorous, confidential; he was immaculate as he had always been, trim, clean-shaven, but his eyes had faded from a coal-bright black to the dull opacity of agates, and his relaxed lower lids were red like blood within.

He said, "Well—Elizabeth Lane! I saw by the paper you were back. I'm glad to have this chance for a word with you."

"I'm glad, too, Cousin Tune. It's like old times."

That was true; meeting him had brought back to the present an older Sunbury. I saw him again in all the places I had ever seen him—in a chair on the sidewalk in front of the Grand Hotel, in the grocer's buying peppermints, in the drugstore lighting his cigar. The town became a background for that figure—strangely, too, because he had been in Sunbury very little, just often enough to present to us all a picture of elegant wickedness laughing, not without tolerance, at dowdy virtue.

"Are you still living at the Grand Hotel?" I asked him.

"Yes." He smiled wryly, as if, after all these years, there seemed to him still something grotesque in the name. "Only it's the 'Regal,' now. But the second-story windows have got the same old cast-iron balconies around 'em."

"Yes, I noticed."

"It's pleasant to have you here again. We're the last of the family in Sunbury. Oh—a distant cousin, here and there, maybe, on a farm. But no Barkalows, and no Van Dorens. All the uncles and aunts are gone."

I murmured, "I know," and thought sorrowfully that the old man had lost all sense of time. *His* uncles and aunts, he had meant, and Grandmother's, the youngest of whom, Uncle Aaron, had been dead a quarter of a century.

"And all the cousins. Libby has been gone how many years now?"

"Libby" was my grandmother. I paused to count back. "Twenty years, anyway."

Then Cousin Tune came back to the present. "Have you seen the Barkalow house?" He eyed me with a half-malicious little smile.

I had seen it—Cousin John Barkalow's house, all its mid-Victorian splendor fallen into ruin: broken iron balconies under broken windows, hanging gutters, weeds as tall as the rusted iron fence. Some forgotten windstorm had knocked a dead tree crashing down against the porte cochere, and it leaned there still in the angle of the wall, its upper branches thrust through a bedroom window.

"Who owns it?"

"Its owner never comes to Sunbury, that I know of. It went to Damaris's boy. You remember she had a son."

A year ago, three thousand miles away, this would

have meant little to me. But I had come home, and standing there on the courthouse square, I remembered Damaris and was moved. Damaris, fleeing from life—gracefully, like a figure in antique myth, like Daphne, or Arethusa, or that fair-ankled Ino who ran into the sea—but fleeing nevertheless, and therefore incomprehensible to all the Barkalow kin.

Cousin Tune moved his stick, gestured with his hat. "I'm glad you're back. You're a writer; maybe you can help me. I'm writing the story of my life."

"Oh, do put it all down." I thought of the rumors I had heard long ago, the whispers eddying in his wake, that had made his life seem to me so romantic, so mysterious. "That's an America that's dead and gone, and it will be lost if those of you who lived it don't get it down in black and white." I didn't say "And soon," although I wanted to. Cousin Tune must be past ninety.

"It won't be a Sunday school story, exactly."

"I know. But people haven't been reading Sunday school stories for a long while now."

"And you will look it over for me? . . . I tell you: why don't you write a book about the old Sunbury? It's dead and gone too. The Sunbury you knew when you were a little girl."

We looked at each other for a moment, and a certain hereditary stubbornness in me went out to meet his own. Our squared chins said "We will put it down: the old times, and all we remember about the places we love, and the people we knew, and so give them a kind of immortality."

For even handwriting on paper, if our words should never be printed, is more enduring than flesh and bone, than brick and beam and plaster. While I live, my grandmother and father live, and all the cousins, even Cousin Cond, whom I never saw; if I write about them they will survive after me so long as the pages survive.

* * *

I shook hands with Cousin Tune again, and wished him luck, and walked away hoping that he would get his book written. I should like to read it. One thing was certain—there would be little about Sunbury in its pages. He had never spent much time there, except that summer when Cousin Cond's son Steven was at Grandmother's and Damaris Barkalow at Cousin John's.

Since the day I saw Cousin Tune on the courthouse square, I have been able to think of nothing but that one summer out of all my summers with Grandmother. I keep seeing Cousin Steve when he laughed, and Damaris Barkalow when she moved, and so this must be a book about them. Cousin Tune will never include in the story of his life his version of that unhappy season, although he was there and saw it happen. Through all my childhood I saw him now and then on the street on those rare occasions when he was in town, but I never missed him when he was gone. That one summer our paths did cross, his and mine, and our doings were concerned with the same end: to make Steve happy.

If it was partly my fault that Steve died, because I felt myself pledged to hold my tongue, and did hold it, at the wrong moment—I know now, and I am not sure but that I knew then—Steve's death was not so sad as the grief, the loss and frustration that he suffered before he died, and that I could do nothing to assuage.

The detached, untroubled mind reflects that so much at least can now be done for Steve and the days of his life in writing about them—but the unreasonable heart remembers how it came near breaking, in the wild, abandoned grief of a child.

Chapter Two

Summer as an entity, eternally the same, is a warm and golden light in the mind. Summers in particular: the memory moves among days and hours and sees them, one after another; moves slowly, circling like a hawk, lazily, until it is all clear to the eye, the ear. One day, one hour: you are back again where you were, and—without knowing why, without knowing quite what it is that moves you—you even feel, in your heartbeat, in your throat, what you felt once before, long ago.

With my mind I can recall that particular summer, when I was living with Grandmother—the emptiness of the upstairs, where no one slept but me, until Steve came. I remember how different an aspect the season wore after he came.

He looked at Sunbury with wonder and delight, as at an ancient cherished dream fulfilled. He saw it with loving eyes, and he taught something new even to me, who had so long known summer there that I could not remember learning it.

Summer meant the opulence of "piney" bushes in full bloom in country graveyards, twilight and the fireflies in tall wheat, afternoon and that same wheat ripened to a pale ash gold, the unfolding banners of the corn, the bright disks of flower on every rose-of-Sharon in every yard in town. One brief season is enough to teach the ear to distinguish in the insect chorus the voice of cricket and locust, of grasshopper and katydid.

But it was Steve who showed me how green a world we lived in. Greenness that I had taken for granted was a revelation to a boy who had known only Texas.

"It's like swimming in deep water," he said, "and the sun's got a long way down to come before it hits bottom."

It was true. Trees rose over the town—buckeye, walnut, tulip; locust, box elder, elm—but the maples outnumbered all the others, and maple boughs hang low and thick between you and the more distant scene. Truly, it was rather like living in a deep green sea. But it was quieter beneath our trees than water could ever be.

It is not hard to remember that quietness. A passing hay wagon was audible the length of the street, the fall of the horses' hooves muffled in dust, the squeak of its wheels a thin, unvarying rhythm.

But remembering so, deliberately and because you choose to, is not remembering with your bones and the flesh on your bones, so that you are transported to another time and are for a moment what and who you were then—in the way I remembered a little while ago, the first week in June, perhaps, soon after I had met Cousin Tune uptown. I came out of the post office to the corner where there is a traffic light today; drowning out oil and gasoline, borne on the gentle wind to that corner, came the fragrance of clover. For a second I did not recognize it; then I thought, "Sunbury is country, still; the fields are just there, beyond." But what I was *being,* even as I thought, was Elizabeth Lane, eleven years old, at the beginning of summer, when the smell of clover hung in the air.

When I was a child the War still explained so much:

the old men with wooden legs who sat in chairs in front of the Grand Hotel, and those with empty sleeves who sold needles and pins from door to door, pencils and matches, and books about "our boys in blue" that no one wanted. The War was the most important and memorable part, the climax of all that had happened to the older people of Sunbury. That I well understood because it held so large a place in my grandmother's mind.

She must have been in her sixties in those years of my childhood, when she so enjoyed telling about her own youth and about times earlier, as she had heard of them from her mother and all her uncles and aunts. I liked to listen, and listening, I kept my eyes so intent on Grandmother that I can see her still as she was then, before she grew really old. She was a bustling little woman who had "settled on her feet," in the country phrase; her hips were wide, her shoulders narrow, her neck and chin tilted forward. But her hair was still dark rather than gray, her eyes were quick and black. She was never idle, but she could talk while she worked.

I knew even then why she generally told her stories in the kitchen: it was because Gran'pa laughed at her when he happened to overhear. By profession a doctor, he too had been a soldier once, like Grandmother's cousins, but he was no great believer in the heroic. Although his eyes were kind and his hands gentle, he was always abrupt in manner, brusque in speech; when Grandmother talked about the War, he would snort and lower his head and look at her over his glasses with twinkling eyes. Dashed and a little shamefaced, she would let her sentences dwindle away to nothing.

Grandmother did not care to be laughed at; so far as I know, no one except Gran'pa ever ventured openly to do so. And in spite of her small size and dumpling shape, no one ever took advantage of her, or tried to, more than once. She had her likes and dislikes, her admirations, her contempts, and she never changed her mind about them; her lips could go straight and thin with disapprobation, she could shake her head implacably. She could excuse much in a blood relation, but not everything: she despised unthrift and laziness. Yet she was capable of a grudging, unacknowledged envy: it was easier for her to forgive the faults of her poor cousins than of the rich ones; it was harder for her to like the John Barkalows than any of the others.

In her stories, relatives living still and relatives long dead alike acted their parts. I knew them all. I knew the soldiers: the ones who had died in battle, like Cousin Jacob Smock, and the ones who had survived, like Cousin Condit Van Doren and his brother Tunis, and Cousin John Barkalow. Cousin Cond I never saw; he had gone to Texas after the War. But Grandmother made him so real to me that I understood her affection for him and why, after he died, she welcomed his son as she did when he came to our house to stay. Cousin Tune was occasionally in Sunbury, but because Grandmother disapproved of him I did not let her know of our friendship, based on his courtesy and his candy and my gratitude. I knew Cousin John Barkalow better: he and Cousin Clara lived in Sunbury alone in the big house at the top of Hill Street, and I saw them every Sunday at church.

Grandmother's religion, I suspect, was bound up with her regard for her family—founded on loyalty as certainly as on conviction. At any rate, it was as inseparable an element of her everyday life as her cooking and housekeeping. After her death, her Bible came to me. One time long afterward, when I picked it up carelessly, little squares of paper, clippings and keepsakes, went fluttering down to the floor from its pages, and I could not help smiling at the picture brought to my mind.

Every winter evening, when the dishes had been washed and put away, Grandmother would come into the sitting room, pull her low rocker into the corner between the table and the fire, and sit with her Bible in her lap while she read the evening paper. Gran'pa always went to bed at nine unless he had been called out to a patient. I solved arithmetic problems at the center table, or studied geography, while Grandmother worked her way through the news. She never leaned back in her rocker, but sat upright, a little round-shouldered, indomitable figure. When she dozed, not infrequently, her head would fall forward, she would breathe heavily; I would watch her with wonder, not daring even to smile; then her head would jerk, or her breath catch, and she would open her eyes, lift her spectacles from the end of her nose, straighten the crumpled pages, or with a wide-awake resolute gesture take her scissors from the work basket on the table beside her. There was always some item in the paper that seemed to her worth keeping. Recipes and knitting and crochet patterns she laid aside to be put into the drawers in the secretary reserved for them. Other clippings she slipped into her Bible: death notices of people she had known, birthday superstitions and weather signs, new ways to clean brass and silver, or to prevent moths, or to rid the kitchen of ants. When she had finished reading the news and cutting out her chosen paragraphs, the paper was folded and put aside, or, if I had done all my lessons, I would squat on the floor beside her and cut it into squares and fold them in spills to be put in the jar on the mantel and used by Gran'pa for lighting his pipe. And Grandmother, the last thing before going to bed, would read a chapter in the Bible.

While she read, she managed to hold it so that the small squares of paper did not fall and float away in every direction. But I had forgotten, when I picked up her Bible so many years afterward, how she had used it, and I had bits of yellowed, fragile newsprint to pick up from the rug, and a scrap or two of tinfoil, and even a tiny old-fashioned valentine, with no name on it. But in spite of the way Grandmother with homely familiarity made her Bible a sort of catchall, she reverenced it profoundly as the Word of God; she always called it The Good Book, in capital letters, and never failed to read her chapter before she went to bed.

* * *

Grandmother was a Presbyterian. The "Old Squire," her grandfather, had brought his family up in that church. As far back as the records went, the Barkalows had been Calvinists. So Grandmother went to church twice on Sunday and generally to prayer meeting on Wednesday. She sent me to Sunday school and thought I should join the church, since then, no matter what wickedness, I might be included among the elect. But she was not a bigot. She never forced her religion on anyone; she never reproved the irreligion of others (Gran'pa, particularly) in the ordinary course of living. I never knew her to make an issue of Presbyterianism until the summer Damaris Barkalow came to live with her grandfather.

Grandmother's family was the family of a patriarch, and to hear about it, all the names falling without hesitation from the accustomed tongue, was like hearing the Bible read aloud: "Now these are the children . . ." or "Now these are the sons of . . ." Her grandfather, the Old Squire, born in New Jersey in 1779, had come west as a young man, with all his family, children and parents, and with his old neighbors, his wagon one in a train of sixty. Many of the neighbors were also cousins: the Dutch families that had lived in New York and New Jersey since the seventeenth century had intermarried through all those generations, not often going outside the church, the tongue, the blood, to unite with the English who lived among them. A stubborn folk, the Dutch: not until the middle of the eighteenth century did they give over spelling in their wills their names and their children's in the Dutch fashion: Adriaen, Theunis, Roelof, Jan . . . Grandmother knew the names and the degree of kinship with each other of all her forebears; she had often seen in her grandfather's house "the great Dutch Bible," which passed from eldest son to eldest son and in his will was always the first mentioned of all its owner's possessions. In it the family records were written long after Dutch had become an unknown tongue to the Barkalows, and for the reading of the Word of God it was of no use at all.

Our cousins John Barkalows were members of "our church." I knew them better than I knew any of the country cousins. And from my earliest days in Sunbury I watched them with a certain fascination, because they had a Cross to Bear, as Grandmother used to phrase it (with a certain satisfaction). Cousin John and Cousin Clara sat alone in their pew, year in and year out; that was the visible evidence of their cross. Their son Ralph had been divorced by his wife a long while since, and had gone away from Sunbury as a consequence of the divorce. Their granddaughter Damaris had been sent to a convent school, and had been permitted by her indifferent father to become a Catholic. In Grandmother's eyes, to have a grandchild turn Catholic was undeniably tribulation.

Cousin Clara, with her marceled white hair and her regal bearing, her diamond rings and earrings, embodied my idea of the word "dowager." I remember once her unbending to tell an anecdote of her childhood in a country parsonage, long before the War. Her father had caught her in the pasture, riding the family milch cow. He led her home by the hand; with his free hand he spanked her all the way, and because he was so tall and she so little, he lifted her off her feet every time he spanked. I could not laugh with the grown-ups at the picture: I was too astonished. I gaped at her, not only because it seemed so incredible, so out of key with what she had become, but because, as Mrs. John Barkalow, she could still remember the country minister's child, and find her amusing.

But however far her way of living had diverged from the code of the manse, she remained a Presbyterian. Like Grandmother, she entertained the Ladies' Aid when it was her turn, and offered her bedrooms for delegates to a Missionary Society meeting, or for visiting missionaries home on leave. No one ever heard from her own lips what she had thought when Damaris had turned Catholic, but neither did anyone suppose that it had seemed to her rather humorous and quite unimportant, as it had to Cousin John. Certainly, now, she would oppose the convent as implacably as he.

I had managed not to be at home on the afternoon of the call, but Grandmother reported it that evening at the dinner table.

Without words Cousin Clara had let it be known that she shared Grandmother's opinion, and believed that bread and water and a locked door would bring the young lady to her senses—that only deference to her husband's authority influenced her to treat Damaris without any suggestion of disapproval.

Grandmother never really liked Cousin Clara, who had too much money, and too much of all that money could buy. She enjoyed the fact that, with Damaris so stubbornly bent on going astray, Cousin Clara was in a position to be offered sympathy, if not advice. But Grandmother was old-fashioned enough to approve the respect shown by his wife for Cousin John's opinions and methods.

"It's as well," she said, "to let a man think he's master."

Gran'pa snorted. "She knows John Barkalow better than you do, Libby."

Grandmother said, "Nonsense. John's too easygoing for his own good, and always has been." I was incredulous, too, because I didn't think anyone, even Cousin John, could successfully oppose Cousin Clara. It was only later that I realized how completely that genial, kind, and mirthful man was master in his own household, and how he followed his own methods to his own ends.

I was not at home the afternoon of the call on Grandmother, but I was in the parlor the day Damaris came for a recipe for piccalilli, or chilli peppers, or something of the kind, for her grandmother. I was there because the minister had dropped in, in the course of his congregational visits, and Grandmother had called me to come and speak to him.

The minister's name, what he was like, what he was saying on that afternoon in June when everyone I knew was outdoors playing, I have long since forgotten. I have a vague picture in my mind of a tall man with a small head and a black mustache and a grave manner; all else is gone. But I do remember the air of constraint in the room after Damaris had come in. She wore a wide-brimmed hat, flat on the top of her head, and perhaps it was that which forced her to sit forward on the edge of her chair, like a half-tamed bird ready to dart away at any threatening gesture. The hat, the ruffles on her lawn frock, her silk parasol; the stiff mahogany rocking chair she perched on, with the spindles up its back; and behind her the glass bookcase doors, reflecting the green light of the out-of-doors, the leaves and the sunshine: those things, in Grandmother's dark, immense parlor, I can still see.

The minister did not stay long to endure Damaris's monosyllabic response to his conversational efforts. Her presence had power enough to make him feel awkward; he said his good-byes rather abruptly. When Grandmother came back from the door, she was prepared to be severe.

"He's a good man," she said, "who wanted to be friendly. . . . It's too bad you were allowed to grow up not knowing your family traditions. A Presbyterian minister has always been a welcome and respected guest in a Barkalow home. We have never—" She held her breath a second, but she couldn't resist saying it. "We have never had much use for Catholics. But there—" she added generously, "it isn't your fault. I blame it on your father and on John Barkalow."

I sat still as a mouse and watched Damaris with caught breath. She seemed to me far too grown-up to be scolded: I was half-frightened by Grandmother's temerity, although I shared her prejudices. I thought of Dutchmen, hundreds of years ago, fighting Alva, enduring the Inquisition, manning the dikes. It was for their sakes that in church I shrilled "I will be true to thee till death" with passionate conviction; I could not imagine being anything but Presbyterian.

Damaris did not protest against the attack; she said nothing. Grandmother sat down again, with no indication that she would ever remember the recipe, or go for it. Damaris had perforce to listen; she sighed and squirmed back a little farther into the seat of her chair, but still she leaned forward, poised for flight, her hand alert on the ivory handle of her parasol.

"I don't know what's got into the young people in this family," Grandmother said. "They're soft. They haven't any grit. They couldn't have come out here in Conestoga wagons, and lived in log cabins until they got their houses built and their land cleared. Why, one of my great-aunts—Aunt Sally Barkalow—I've heard her tell it many a time. She was Sally Hendrickson before she married. Back in Jersey she was doing the washing one Monday morning, and her beau came round—Uncle Art Barkalow, Grandfather's brother—and he said, 'Sally, if you want to marry me, come along—we're leaving for Ohio this evening.' 'Twas the first she'd heard of it, she said—men didn't consult their women-folks much in those days. And there she was, up to her elbows in suds. But she left her clothes in the tub for her mother to finish, and wiped her arms and rolled her sleeves down, and went with him to the preacher's house. I don't see any of you setting out for the wilderness without any notice. Or doing a family washing either, for that matter."

Damaris laughed, but her voice was faintly resentful as she replied. "Cousin Libby, I think I could do a washing. I mean—it isn't as if I were afraid of work. The Sisters work—hard."

"And they were all," Grandmother went on firmly, as though now she had arrived at the point she wanted to make, and was not to be diverted, "they were all honest, upright Presbyterians. They stood up to their God. Like Job. And when they sinned, they knew it, and they had it out with Him. They didn't need a priest, or any saint, for a go-between."

No doubt Grandmother had very strange ideas of the Catholic Church: she knew as little about it at sixty-five as I did at eleven. She may even have feared that she would make herself ridiculous in Damaris's sight, for she said no more about what she supposed Catholics believed, but returned abruptly to her forebears. It was the method she had used with me, so often—holding her ancestors up as models: "They made America. Now you must go on from where they left off."

She said, "Do you know what the first thing was they did when they got out here? They hardly waited to get settled—they hadn't been here long enough to get their houses built before they applied to the district synod to organize a church. And to get their church built, they each contributed part of it. Grandfather's share was the weatherboarding. I've heard him tell it many a time. And each family had to supply its own bench. Of course that building is gone long ago, but the church is there—the Jersey Presbyterian, they call it still. It's brick now, with stained-glass windows. Sometime when we're all out to Uncle Aaron's I'll show it to you."

I doubt if all this made any impression on Damaris. When she could, she reminded Grandmother that she had come on an errand, and when she had the recipe in her hand, she said good-bye and fled. But I remembered it, and long afterward I appreciated Grandmother's "They stood up to their God." The religious attitude of our forefathers comes out quite clearly in their wills, the wording of which reveals over and over again the confidence, the calm faith that sustained them to the end of life. Those wills begin, all or most of them, with the same untroubled preamble: "Principally and first of all I give and recommend my Soul unto the hands of God that gave it, and my Body I recommend to the Earth . . . nothing doubting but at the General Resurrection I shall receive the same again by the mighty power of God; and as touching those worldly things and Estates wherewith it has pleased God to bless me in this life, I give, Devise and Dispose of . . ." It had pleased God to bless most of those honest farmers—"yeomen" or "gentlemen"—with comfortable estates and they were grateful to Him.

* * *

Sometimes I too looked from our pew across to Cousin Clara and Cousin John, and was sorry for them because Damaris had betrayed them and all her ancestors. Then she was brought to Sunbury to live with her grandfather, and so on Sunday mornings I thought of her, and wondered how she could bear to have cut herself off from something so known and familiar—the church and all its congregation. When I came to know her a little I was moved by her solitariness. She walked alone. I felt, in some dim way, that in Sunbury at least, however it may have been at the convent, she must feel alien in the Catholic Church, since none of her forebears had ever been within its walls. It was a long while before I came to see that she had no feeling of kinship with those of her name who had gone before her, that she felt at home only in the Church that had tutored her childhood.

I had sometimes seen Damaris walking with her light step in the shade of the maple trees in front of Cousin John Barkalow's. Ruffled dimity dress, wide hat, grave mouth and dark eyes—mysterious, remote, and strange—and fascinating in the same awful way as a young person known to be doomed to an early death. For Damaris wanted to be a nun. She did not know me then, and I could stare, while my heartbeat quickened. And in the air, under the dark trees, drifted that same honey-sweet scent of clover fields.

I know that when I saw her those first few times, she was always alone. As the summer went on, Cousin Clara must have "entertained" for her; there were times when the Barkalow tennis courts were full, and there were evenings when Damaris sat on whichever front porch the young people had chosen, and with them sang the summer's new songs to mandolin and guitar. But those times never erased from my mind that first impression I had of Damaris walking alone. Once, when I was on my way to catch minnows in the creek, I saw her on horseback, in derby hat and flowing habit. There was something romantic and glamorous in the sight; I wondered where she could have spent the summers when she had not been in Sunbury.

It was natural enough, really, for Damaris to want to be a nun. She had been a child when her father had sent her to the convent school. It was the somewhat ironical custom of our country, in those days, to dispose in that way of the daughters of broken homes. Their families took it for granted that they would for a while want to enter the Catholic Church; the desire was laughed at: like measles, it was a self-limited disease.

Whether Cousin John believed that Sunbury's atmosphere of the commonplace would cure Damaris of her fantastic whim; whether she hoped to wheedle permission out of him, that she had come so submissively and with so good a grace; which of them would triumph—I think I did not even wonder at the time. But from a distance I regarded my cousin with half-frightened awe because she had a part in rites and mysteries I should never know, but which I assumed were altogether dark.

Damaris was slight and fair-skinned, small-boned, tight-knit, with a waist a boy's hands could easily encircle. Her hair, worn in a loose knot on the nape of her neck, was bright like amber, golden or brown according to the light on it. Her eyes were dark—the black Barkalow eyes—in a small pointed face. She was quiet in all her ways and quick in all her movements—too quick, almost breathless. Many years later I thought of Damaris when I read of Daphne or Ino in the poets. But I recognized in her manner, even as a child, without knowing the words for it, something shy and wary, quick to evade.

* * *

Sometimes I wish that I could go back thirty years, and argue with Grandmother and the rest of the family. How could Damaris have felt any kinship with her ancestors? Their names, their ways were sticks used to beat her with. And the disruption of her own family must have seemed to separate her from the past. There could have been little significance for her in stories of her grandfathers.

From the very beginning there was that difference between her and Steve. He came to Sunbury like one who has been in exile all his life; that feeling for his father's home and his father's people was all his heritage from his father, poor Cousin Cond. Then, too, Steve had from the first the approval of his elders. Grandmother would have pitied and loved him in the beginning, whatever he had been, because he came to her almost directly from his father's deathbed.

And Cond was a part of the great family always spoken of by Grandmother as the Aunts and Uncles. Only a few were still living, very old, on scattered farms in the country. I knew them all—not as persons, but as figures, remote and beyond life. For me only one of them was really alive: the youngest son, Grandmother's uncle Aaron, who was only a few years older than she. He had never married, but had lived on the home place and farmed it for his father until the Old Squire died. He had inherited it from that just patriarch, who had established his other sons in life when they were young men.

Summer in my memory is summer on that farm, as well as at Grandmother's. There were no children in the house when I knew it; Cousin Anne, one of Uncle Aaron's unmarried nieces, lived there and kept house for him. It was so quiet, and so hot—there were no stories in the bookcases—one could only dream of the past. Now, in my mind, all the pasts are merged; there is one great golden summer: the Squire's, Uncle Aaron's, Grandmother's, and mine. And Steve's. But never Damaris's. She had been cheated of her share in it.

It must have been in June that Cousin Steve first came to our house. When I try to remember when it was, the warm fragrance of cooking strawberries comes back to my mind, and I am in the summer kitchen again, and the date is fixed for me.

Cousin Anne Barkalow and Grandmother were putting up the strawberries, and I was helping them. All day long the syrupy, cloying perfume of the cooking berries hung thick about us in the summer kitchen. The berry patch was Cousin Anne's: every year she sold Grandmother enough for the winter's preserves, and then spent the day at our house helping with them. I hulled the berries while Grandmother stirred the kettle on the big wood-burning summer range, and Cousin Anne filled the mason jars on the table, screwed their tops on, and wiped them clean. My back was turned to the two women; I made myself as unobtrusive as I could, and they talked as if I had not been there.

All the strange, sad deaths that old people are doomed to die they encompassed in their gossip, and I listened in fascinated horror. In the parlor I might have been less moved, because in there, at their leisure, Grandmother and Cousin Anne would have sat rocking with handkerchiefs in their hands, and would have wept a little as familiar names fell from their tongues. But in the strawberry-scented summer kitchen they were too busy for tears, their tones were brisk, their exclamations of grief and sympathy no more heartfelt than those of pain and annoyance when a finger was burned or a kettle boiled over. They were saying, mutely but nonetheless clearly, "Well—what can you expect? Life is like that."

I thought with a sinking heart, "Life is like that," and I was frightened for Grandmother and Cousin Anne.

Then Cousin Anne turned the conversation to the John Barkalows. She had seen Damaris, who had driven out to the farm with her grandfather on some errand: something about a horse to ride.

"A good strong wind," said Cousin Anne firmly, "would blow that girl away."

"Like an autumn leaf," Grandmother agreed, "and not much greater loss."

"Seems funny to me Ralph's wife didn't get that girl. She got the divorce, didn't she? On account o' that to-do about . . . about that woman."

"She didn't ask for the custody of the child. That was John's doing."

"I always heard tell he bought her off."

"So they said. You can't imagine John letting any of his flesh and blood get away from him, can you? I

always did think Ralph's wife was a cold-blooded creature, but imagine it . . ." Grandmother tchked and shook her head. "Her own child."

Perhaps they had really forgotten my presence. Who did they mean by "that woman"? I had never known so much as this about Damaris before. I felt a shock of pity at Grandmother's words, and a comprehension, due to my love for my mother and my sureness of her love for me, of Damaris's plight: who would not be lost and frightened out in the open world beyond a convent's gates, if you knew your mother had *sold you?* I sat and thought about Damaris—wondered if she knew.

Then Cousin Anne, apparently still thinking of money, or the lack of it, said, "And there was Cond. How was he off? Did he leave anything to those five boys? There was five, wasn't there?"

Grandmother had had word from one of Cousin Cond's sons early in the spring, an almost illiterate note from the Texas ranch, announcing Cond's death: "This is to advise you that Pop passed away Monday, after a painful sickness. He was buried yesterday. He wanted that you should know."

"I never knew a thing about him after he went to Texas," she said.

* * *

A while after that, we heard the footsteps of men on the path outside and saw their figures through the lattice. I knew by the white suit that one of them was Cousin Tunis Van Doren. There was a boy, tall, awk-

ward, and shy, behind him at whom I hardly glanced, because I was so glad to see Cousin Tune.

I thought: "Like a story, he comes in on the talk about his brother." When he stopped at the foot of the steps where I was sitting, I held out my hand, and then I remembered in time how sticky and stained it was and jerked it back to wipe it on the apron that enveloped me. He laughed, but he did take off his hat and bow, too. His bow was one of the things I loved him for. Now he kept his wide-brimmed panama hat and his cane in one hand, while with the other he commenced feeling through the pockets of the linen jacket he wore, for the peppermints he always carried.

"Is your grandmother about, Elizabeth?"

"Grandmother," I said without turning, "here's Cousin Tune." The announcement was not necessary; I knew she must have seen him from her place by the stove.

"Howdy, Tune. How are you? What brings you here?" and then she added, a little shamefacedly, "To the back door, I mean."

"No one came when I knocked—and I smelled preserves." He smiled, amused, and his eyes twinkled. "So I knew you were home, and I particularly wanted to see you. I have a surprise for you, Libby."

The boy with Cousin Tune had stopped short of the steps, with the lattice between him and Grandmother. Now she came over to stand behind me, where she could see him. Grandmother stood with her arms crossed, the jam ladle, still in one hand, outthrust and dripping in long slow syrupy drops. She said nothing, but as she waited there she caught her breath, her eyes

widened. Her mouth was straight, severe. She pointed the ladle.

"Who is that?"

Cousin Tune reached out and laid a hand on the boy's arm, drew him forward. He had snatched off his hat. A long curled lock of hair hung over his left eyebrow. His face, tanned and leathery though it was, grew uncomfortably flushed. His mouth was unsteady. Cousin Tune said, "It's Cond's youngest son. I brought him back from Texas with me for a visit."

Grandmother laughed then, rather uncertainly. "Goodness me, Tune, you startled me out of my wits. I didn't know you'd been to Texas. . . . He's the spittin' image of you at that age. I thought mebbe you'd raised a family unbeknownst to any of us."

"Cond and I always looked alike, except that he was taller."

"Yes, I remember—" Then she broke off to invite them into the summer kitchen, to make the boy welcome, to apologize because she could not leave her jam. She sent me to bring chairs from the kitchen, and the two men sat down, back in the corner, out of the way—leaned against the lattice and were haloed by the sun outside so that I could not see their faces clearly.

Grandmother and Cousin Anne returned to their work. I went back to the step and picked up the crock of strawberries still to be hulled. Grandmother talked to the boy for a moment about his journey: made him easy and comfortable. The flush faded from his high cheekbones; I saw what a thin face he had, with lines deep from nose to mouth. But his eyes were happy, like a grateful child's, and his smile made you want to touch

his knee, to reassure him. I had no adjectives then for that boyish smile of Steve's; I know them now—deprecating, wistful, ingratiating—yet even they do not say it, exactly; it was a smile that asked, sweetly and humbly, for affection.

I was so intent, trying to see him clearly against his sunny background, saying to myself, with ecstasy, "Texas cowboy," that I paid little heed, at first, to the conversation. But certain facts must have been learned then, for afterward I knew them: Steve had four brothers who were much older than he; his mother was dead and had been for many years; the ranch was mortgaged, and anyway it would hardly take care of them all; he wasn't much of a hand with cattle, although he had a knack with horses. He'd come back to Ohio to stay with his uncle while he looked for something to do.

Grandmother sniffed at that. "Heaven knows what you'd find if you stood at Tune's elbow to look for it. Besides, he isn't fixed for visitors. The Grand Hotel!—when he's in Sunbury, which is seldom, I must say. No, you must come and stay with us until you find work. Afterward, too, if you like. Your father was like a brother to me once, and after all—" she paused to look him over, slowly, "you're like him, like he was before the War."

"Do you think there's many opportunities in Sunbury?" Cousin Tune sounded sarcastic, but nevertheless I knew he was pleased: even then I could see that he was ready to turn his nephew over to Grandmother, perhaps had brought him there with that intention.

"There's more chance for him here than he'd find in White Lick Springs, or those places you go to."

Then I heard Grandmother ask Cousin Anne if

maybe Uncle Aaron could give Steven work on the farm, as a hand.

"He might, at threshing season. He always needs help with the threshing."

I said, "Maybe Cousin John Barkalow'd give him a place."

Grandmother turned to me sharply, cross as an adult is sometimes when a child quite innocently makes an unfortunate remark. "He's not going to ask his cousin John for work."

Cousin Tune laughed shortly. "Cond would roll over in his grave."

Grandmother had had enough of my presence. "Elizabeth, haven't you finished with those berries? Well—set them up, anyway. It's time you were getting cleaned up."

But before I had put the crock on the table and taken my apron off, the men were on their feet, too. Steve would go back with Cousin Tune to the hotel for his grip. Grandmother made him promise to return for supper; in the meantime, she would fix a bedroom for him. He was more than welcome to come and stay as long as he liked.

When they had gone, the man and the boy, Grandmother and Cousin Anne, without comment, returned to the strawberries. In the summer kitchen the light came farther and farther through the lattice, over the floor and onto the stove, so that it was hotter there than it had been all day long, and the two women were in a hurry to be done. When the strawberries were all in their jars, upside down in rows on the table, Gran'pa came through from the house and stopped in the door from the kitchen long enough to ask when he could have some supper. Grandmother went down cellar to get the cream pitcher and the butter crock out of the tin safe; Cousin Anne cut the bread and I got up from my place on the step to lay out thin slices of ham on the green platter.

* * *

The sun was low behind the house next door; we were all in shadow, and the grape arbor was a dusky tunnel. Beyond it, though, there was sunlight still; old Cousin Bias had the hose out and was watering the garden when Steve returned. The water made a rainbow in the sun over the row of cabbages, and you could smell the fresh dampness as far as the summer kitchen. Bias Van Doren, who was no relation to Grandmother but a first cousin of Cousin Tune's, had been so wounded in the War that one leg was afterward shorter than the other, and he walked with a sideways lunge and lurch, one shoulder forward and his head down. Grandmother still called him Tobe, but since the War, the town had called him Bias. He was a little cracked, but an able handyman.

Steve put his valise down on the step, saying, "Just let me speak to him, then I'll be right in."

I watched him go down the grape arbor to its end. Bias looked at him stupidly while he talked, then flung the hose aside, wiped his hand on the seat of his overalls, and gave it to Steve to shake. In the end, the two of them walked away across the yard. Steve came back alone. It was he who remembered to turn off the water at the hydrant. When he picked up his valise he was looking flushed and uncomfortable, a little defiant.

"I couldn't help but feel sorry for him. It's tough when all your relations have everything."

"If you mean you have everything," Grandmother smiled at him, "you're pretty easy satisfied."

"Pop always said," and he smiled back at her doubtfully, "his cousin Tobias never had a chance, 'cause his mother wasn't a Barkalow."

Grandmother was pleased. "Grandfather Barkalow always looked after his own, I will say. I hope that's still in the blood." And she added, in a gentler tone, "I'm glad to have your father's boy here, Steven. You can be sure this is home to you as long as you like."

It was easy to love Steve from the very first. I went to sleep that night hoping that he would stay with us always.

* * *

When Steve came to Sunbury to make his fortune, like one of the boys in McGuffey's *Readers*, Cousin John's house on the hill was the most opulent and pompous of all the big houses in town, and it was to Cousin John that McGuffey's *Readers* boys applied, but I think it did not occur to anyone but me that Steve might do so. After he had spent a week or two in town vainly looking for work, I began to fear that he must go to the farm as Cousin Anne had suggested, and ask to be taken on as one of Uncle Aaron's hands.

I thought he didn't go out to the farm to ask for work because he was frightened of being confined there. It was later when I saw that it was not so much reluctance on Steve's part that kept him in town as it was the unwillingness of Cousin Tune to let him seek the country, and I realized that since his uncle had brought him to Sunbury, a certain deference to that uncle's wishes was a repayment he could make. For a while, at least, without any real passion for moneymaking to drive him, Steve had to spend at least part of every day searching the town over for an employer.

Cousin Tune had come to sit on our porch one night—a startling enough departure from his custom in the first place. He always spent his evenings in one of the chairs outside the hotel, tipped back against the iron bar across the window, his hat over one eye, his feet crossed, his cigar dangling from his fingers.

It was nearing the end of June. There were fireflies in the long grass, and in the air, and crawling on the leaves of the lilac bushes. I sat on the steps and caught those that came drifting past, and dropped them into an onion top I had gone to the garden for. Gran'pa was there, too, and he and Cousin Tune were smoking cigars, and, for the most part, talking politics. The scent of the tobacco smoke was heavy in the quiet air, and the odor of onion was sharp in my nostrils, and the lightning bugs left their own queer smell on the tips of my fingers. From where I sat on the step I could see a bat swooping darkly between the trees. Down street, on another porch, there was music: mandolin, guitars, and young voices, girls' and boys'. I wished I were old enough for the boys to bring guitars to my porch. I felt deserted. That was where Steve was, on that other porch, singing cowboy songs to some girl in dimity ruffles.

Cousin Tune was saying, interrupting Gran'pa and something about the tariff: "Is that Steve singing, Libby? That's good for him: he's never known any girls in his life. . . . I wonder if he's met his cousin Damaris on any of these porches?"

Grandmother sniffed. "He will, sooner or later, when she forgets she's dedicated her life to the Pope. I can't see why you shouldn't be glad to have him safe on Uncle Aaron's farm while she's about."

Gran'pa laughed. "Libby, you take it for granted he'll fall in love with her at first sight, just because she's John Barkalow's. I should hope the boy's got better sense. I grant you she's an appealing young'un, but I should think he could see she's a walkin' invitation to every germ that sees her."

"I've never heard of her being sick," Grandmother said tartly. "And if I know the breed, she won't be, until she's safe married. Then she'll probably be an invalid all the rest of her life "

"A well-established invalid, anyway." Cousin Tune was cynical.

Grandmother attacked him again on the subject of the farm. "Mind you, Tune, I'm pleased as can be to have Steven here. I'm fond of him, just like I was always fond of his father. But there's nothing for him in town, and it's a do-less kind of existence for the boy. Bad for him. What's your objection to the farm?"

"He's lived all his life away from people; he needs to meet a few."

"He'll meet Damaris Barkalow."

"Besides, I'd like to see him amount to something. Where's being a farmhand going to get him?"

"Farming was good enough for your ancestors, Tunis Van Doren, if it wasn't good enough for you."

Grandmother was angry, really angry, and because I was fond of Cousin Tune I wanted to say something—

anything—in a hurry. What I said was an echo of my romantic pleasure in the thought that Steven and Damaris were the heirs of a family feud.

"Didn't Cousin Anne say Damaris was going horseback riding on the farm this summer?"

Cousin Tunis moved sharply: I could hear his rockers scrape on the floor. I didn't look round from my place on the step, against the post. I didn't dare.

"That hothouse flower?" he chuckled. "I don't believe even John Barkalow could get her on a real, live horse."

"Oh, she does ride horseback," I insisted, "I've seen her."

I thought then of how strong Damaris could seem, at times. I thought of her—proud and unbending—walking through Sunbury. Knowing what had happened—"that woman," her mother *selling* her, coming to Cousin John's as though she were orphaned—from then on, whenever I saw her criticized, I defended Damaris Barkalow. I thought of her invisible father, Ralph. And how she had learned something I then admired so much—strength for oneself.

"Maybe not a hothouse flower, then," Tune conceded. "Maybe just a water hyacinth. No roots, that's the trouble with that girl. No good strong roots in a good solid soil. Pity she couldn't have had you for a grandmother, Libby."

I said anxiously, "D'you think I've got roots, Cousin Tune?"

"Trust your grandmother." He chuckled. "Honey, you've got roots like that trumpet vine on the gate. Cut it down, but unless you take a pickax to its roots, it'll be back. Maybe halfway across the lawn, where you least want it, but it'll be back."

Grandmother h'mphed. "You're a good one to talk about roots, Tune Van Doren, I must say."

"I come back, don't I?" And then he added, in a tone that managed to be conciliatory and mocking at the same time, "Of course you're right, Libby. Save him from a life like mine. Get him out to the Old Place, and let him have a look at it. After all, it's not much like Texas, and that's what he needs to get away from. We'll see, presently, what he really wants."

Then suddenly I hoped with all my heart that Steve would not fall in love with Damaris—would not meet her, even. Because Steve was real and not the hero of a ballad, and I loved him and wanted him to be happy. I can't be sure, now, why one brief glimpse that I had of Damaris, myself unnoticed, was so enlightening, why it made me so sure that she had the power to make him suffer. But I remember that it was so, that I saw her, that I knew.

It was Sunday and one of those cool, windy mornings we sometimes have in June, with the treetops tossing light as air, dust whirling in eddies at street corners, and tall clouds leaning like the tower of Pisa across a fathomless blue sky. I was on my way to Sunday school, my pigtails tidy, my blue sash neatly tied, my starched embroidered petticoats rebellious in the wind. From the corner where I had to cross, I saw Damaris coming up Main Street from the West End. She had been to eight o'clock Mass, I thought, remembering the bells. Hers was the only figure in that long block; it seemed somehow unbearably lonely.

The wind was twisting her skirts as it twisted mine; she held them with one hand and her wide hat with the other as she walked with her head down. She moved swiftly, as always, and gracefully; the shadows of the maple trees touched her and no more as she passed beneath them. When she came into the sun, the light glittered on the gold crucifix that hung on her rosary; with every step it swung heavily from side to side, pendulumwise, from breast to breast. Her hat was so wide, her head so bent, that when she paused at the corner I could see only the lower half of her face. Her mouth was quiet, grave and sweet, like the Sisters I had seen.

When Sunday school was over, I went into the church auditorium and slipped into Grandmother's pew without waiting for her. After the service began, after "Praise God from whom all blessings flow" and the first hymn, I could settle back to think of Damaris, and ask what it was about her that seemed so foreboding, and why Steve mustn't love her. They were unanswerable questions, but I felt conscience-stricken, as if my careless wishing him in love had made grief and sorrow his portion. A cold hand on my backbone made me shiver.

Chapter Three

By that time Steve no longer seemed a visitor at Grandmother's. He lived with us. Much of the time he was away from the house, looking for a job in the town, hobnobbing in the hardware store with farmers and farmhands, asking for work everywhere but at Cousin John's factory. When he was away I too let the gate swing shut behind me and went with the boys and girls to woods and creek banks, or ran up and down the alleys playing noisy games. But when he was at home I never left him.

One day when he had come back from his search for work, unsuccessful as usual, I asked him what he really wished he could do. I emphasized "wished" because although I knew Uncle Aaron would give him a place on the farm any day he asked for it, I was curious, like Cousin Tune, about his secret desires.

And he said, "Write poetry."

I suppose that my jaw dropped. I remember how he flushed. I gaped up at him, and said, "You mean you—just want to, someday—or you *do?*"

I hope that I sounded awed; at any rate, Steve was pleased, and began fumbling in his hip pocket for his notecase. Truly, I was awed, not by the fact that he was a poet—I am afraid that seemed to me uncomfortable, it was so incongruous—but by his ability to speak of it so easily, so casually. To write poetry was my own secret ambition, but I would have had my tongue cut out rather than admit it. Steve was a shy boy; I am sure he could not have confided his foolishness to Grandmother or anyone else. And I am glad that never while he lived did I mention his desire, his ambition, to anyone. It was not only a sense of shared confidence that made me hold my tongue; I am afraid that I was ashamed for him. As it happened, if he was hungering for praise, he received little comfort from me; I listened to his verses in silence, because I loved him too much to say what I thought.

My knowledge of poetry was limited to the contents of our school readers and a few old books like the "Percy" on Gran'pa's shelves. Poetry that wasn't simple I didn't read, beyond the first line.

Steve's poetry was simple enough, but like the poetry I knew in nothing else. He took it out of his pocketbook and unfolded it. The pages had been torn from a cheap composition book; they had thin blue lines, and were written over with pencil; the creases were rubbed and soiled, worn through. He read the verses aloud to me, first. Grammar and diction were unconventional, but that was natural to Steve; in his slow, drawling voice what he said sounded right, for him, and he could make the lines move evenly by slurring, by emphasis. But when I took them in my own hand and read them to myself, I knew that by my standards they were not poetry at all. The lines rhymed, two by two, but they had no certain rhythm. Not poetry—yet for some reason I did suddenly and quite clearly see Texas. Not as I had imagined it, but even larger—illimitable, drained of all color by a sun that was the only thing one could put one's mind to, that one couldn't get out of one's head.

Because I was tongue-tied against praise, I talked

about Texas. I asked him why, if he didn't like Texas, he wrote about it.

He said, "Because it's all I know to write about."

I assured him comfortably that now he knew Sunbury, he could write about that. About the trees that he liked so much. I understood better about the trees since I had had that vision of the Texas sun.

"I've not made up a poem since I been here." He carefully refolded the pages I had given back to him and put them away. He said stubbornly that he didn't know Sunbury to write about, only to feel at home in. It was something like Heaven, he reckoned, with a sheepish grin; when you got there you were liable to feel at home, only you wouldn't want to write poems about it for a spell—not until you were sure those already there felt all right about your being there too. "They might think you were takin' too much on yourself."

Later, I could see that Steve had loved Sunbury from the first. Whenever he came into the yard and let the iron gate clang shut behind him, he would put out his hand and lay his palm for an instant on the trunk of the tulip tree that grew there. It was as if he could not quite believe his eyes, but I did not at once and entirely see the meaning of that gesture. I assumed he was being heroic in covering his homesickness for Texas; I didn't know then, in the beginning, that he wanted to get as far from Texas as he could, and to forget it.

I can imagine it now. Steve's brothers were all grown men when he was still a child; his mother had died when he was small; his only real companion had been his aging father. And Cousin Cond, like other old men, must surely have known longing for the past. He was a long, long way from Sunbury and his youth, and as time passed, what his stories lost in truth they would gain in glamour. And so Steve came to Ohio as to a promised land, and grief waited for him. Not through disillusion but through his perfect, childlike, mistaken confidence that there, in the country he had always heard of as "back home," nothing could happen to him that he wanted not to happen: nothing sorrowful, nor disappointing.

I said, "But doesn't this country seem awfully small to you?"

"Yes, it's small, but it's got loving-kindness." He flushed again. "That's a Bible word, isn't it? Good as any, I reckon. But whether that's for everyone—strangers an' all—"

"Well," I said, sensible, "I thought it was people had 'loving-kindness.' I don't know about just fields. But if we go to Uncle Aaron's soon, you can tell. You'll like it, I know."

That much at least I had learned: he would like the Barkalow farm because the house was very old, and deep-buried in trees, as the town and the fields were quiet and peaceful.

* * *

Uncle Aaron had preserved the farm as he had inherited it; I am sure that in his time nothing had altered very greatly. The house was weathered stone, a creamy yellow once, greenish here and there with moss and damp. Its front door was set deep in a recessed porch between the two front rooms: Cousin Anne's parlor and parlor-bedroom. Over the porch was a peaked gable with a round window in its center. The other windows, sunk in thick stone walls, were small and many-paned, and shuttered within. The faded green outside shutters were open, lashed back to the walls by rampant trumpet vine and honeysuckle.

These two front rooms were dark and cool all summer long. Behind them the rest of the house lay exposed; from sunrise to sunset, the light moved across faded carpets and wallpaper, steel engravings, old rocking chairs, and empty fireplaces. In the heat, all the scents of field and barnyard came with the sun; the sounds of birds and insects, of men and horses, were never shut out.

The Old Place stood at the top of a long, gentle slope; I knew it as only a child can know the places where he is at home, with a feeling for their essential quality in his heart and mind, in his very bones and blood. That farm was so perfectly the embodiment of an everlasting peace that it was hard to remember, sometimes, that all its grandsons had gone away to war, with only John Barkalow returning, stronger for his experience, with vitality enough to make the most of the good times coming.

When Steven went with us to spend the day, he was seeing his father's grandfather's home as his father had known it when he was a boy—as his father perhaps had described it, so unlike Texas: the green slope of hill between road and house with the driveway at one side and the single magnificent walnut tree just inside the gate; the old-fashioned pink moss roses in bloom everywhere; the great double chimneys, one at each end; and the settled, overgrown look of the whole place, with its vines and tall bushes and the massive trees all about and overhead. It must have seemed very old to anyone thinking of age and time and the past.

Although I was confused by Steve's poetry, Texas was still a romantic name to my ears; I wanted to hear more about it, and I wanted to see a lasso in the hands of the only one of my cowboy cousins I'd ever be likely to know. At dinner that day, all the family was there. Uncle Aaron was drinking his tea from a saucer held in both hands, his hands gnarled and stiff, with soil ground into them. After stroking his beard for a long time, he said to Steve, "Tell you what you can do; there's a filly I'm pasturing for John Barkalow, that he wants broke. He bought her for his granddaughter to ride. How'd you like to finish the job—teach her her paces?"

"Reckon I could," Steve drawled, indifferently. And though he didn't smile, he couldn't keep his lips from twitching. His whole body came alive, or seemed to, even if he didn't move beyond gripping the table edge with his fingers. "Horses are different from cattle. They got sense. How much does your filly know?"

"She's broke to bit and bridle and saddle, but nobody's been on her back yet. Borry a pair o' overalls out o' my lot, an' come along so's I can show you where the saddle is, in the barn. I got to get back to the cornfield."

Impatient as I was, I could not go along to the barn with Steve and Uncle Aaron. I stayed to carry the dishes to the kitchen for Cousin Anne and Grandmother to scrape and wash. It was my duty to wipe them, pile them up, and put them away. When I was dismissed, I flew out the kitchen door ahead of the two women, to the fence at the edge of the bluff above the barn lot.

Even though I had heard Uncle Aaron say that she was half-broken, I was disappointed to see them standing there so calmly, the boy twisting his hand in the filly's mane and whispering in her ear, while she shook her head and, with dribbling lips, played with the apple he held for her. I called, "Hi, Steve! Let's see you!" But I didn't believe that it was going to be exciting after all.

He waved his hand to me without turning to look, untied the reins from the fence post, and jumped to her back. She reared and plunged. My heart turned over; I caught my breath. When Grandmother and Cousin Anne came to stand nearby, I scarcely noticed them. But when a third person stepped quietly through the grass and weeds, and stopped there beside me, I turned to look. It was Damaris.

The filly rose on her hind legs until it seemed as if she must go over backward. I said hello to Damaris, and looked away from her again to watch Steve, to see that he didn't fall. Her presence was of no comparable importance; and yet, to this day, I can see her standing there, leaning with the rest of us on that weathered silver-gray fence rail. She had a wide white hat that drooped around her face, but she was so much taller than I that I could see her dark, shy, excited eyes, her flushed cheeks, her parted lips. She wore a dress with ruffles on the shoulders, and ruffles round the bottom of her skirt and on the petticoat whose edge was lifted by the stout weeds she stood among.

Damaris said, "So that's our Wild West cousin." And then, after a pause, both of us staring down at the scene in the barnyard, she exclaimed, "Oh, she's beautiful!"

The filly stood on her nose, on her tail; she gathered all four feet under her and jumped and whirled and twisted. I thought she was beautiful, too, but I thought that Steve was magnificent. He stayed in the saddle, moving his heels from her shoulders to her flanks; he held the reins in one hand, and slapped her now and then with the strap he carried in the other.

"He's teasing her," Damaris whispered. "How cruel! But he can ride. He's marvelous."

He was marvelous: graceful and easy and sure. Even the overalls, so much too large for him, failed to make him ridiculous.

"He's wonderful," I said.

"Texas—and no end to riding. I envy him."

"So do I." But I could hardly believe that she did, really. The dimity ruffles belied her words. Although, stealing a glance at her, I could see that she was breathless, that her eyes were dilated and shone.

While Steve's performance lasted, I watched in a dreadful and pleasurable suspense; but I knew even then that in part, at least, it was a performance put on by him for my benefit. No one would mount a horse he couldn't manage in so small and cluttered a space. When the filly edged herself, inch by inch, toward the barn's wide overhang, where Steve's brains might have been knocked out, he was off her back and on his feet again in an instant. He let her run free for an interval, tossing her head, snorting, kicking up her heels; then he took a coiled rope from a fence post, whirled it about his shoulders, let it slide through his fingers, and caught one of her forelegs in the noose. That brought her up standing, all atremble. Before we could see how he did it, he was on her back again, the rope free, whirling about his head as she reared once more. Then she began to circle the strawstack, on two feet, on four, on two again. When they passed the gate, which was not fastened, Steve kicked it, and it swung open. They came round again. Steve tossed his rope away with a triumphant whoop and headed her through the gate. At once they were off, headlong, in a wild run, through the bugloss to the creek, across the creek with a noisy splash and scramble, then up and over the green hill pasture on the other side.

"That's the end," Damaris said.

"Yes." I supposed she meant the end of our Wild West show. "But it was good as Buffalo Bill. And now pretty soon you can ride her."

"That's what I mean. Poor pretty thing! She's been free up to now, and she never will be again." I suppose I looked stupid. "Don't you see: she's been whole—complete in herself—now she isn't. She'll never be happy again without a master; she'll be afraid."

"But horses aren't any good till they're broken. I mean—they aren't intended to be wild."

"No, I suppose not." She smiled a little ruefully. "Well—Gran'pa got a bargain when he bought her. And it will be fun to have a good mare to ride, in place of livery stable horses."

Steve looked up to wave to me as he crossed the barnyard, stopped short in his tracks when he saw a stranger, then went on more slowly to the barn. We could hear his footsteps echo in its emptiness; we turned to the door to meet him. It seemed a long while before he came up the ladder and through the hole in the floor. He had taken off the overalls, but his shirt was soaking wet and clinging to his shoulders, and his one unruly lock of hair was down in his eye. He looked unhappy and self-conscious, like a schoolboy caught in something silly.

"Come on, Steve. This is your cousin Damaris Barkalow. You know—" I said awkwardly, inexperienced in the manner of introductions.

"I know, sure. The filly's yours. Say, I'm sorry I showed off like that. I mean—I didn't know you came—I was showin' 'Liz'beth—"

"Of course; she wanted to see you ride. But I liked it too; and you did break her for me. Thanks a lot." She held out her hand.

"I'm not fit to shake hands. And don't go thankin' me yet awhile. She won't let a lady ride her for a spell. I'll let you know when she's ready."

"Thank you." They started to walk together toward the house; I followed after. "She's going to make a lovely saddle mare, isn't she? But it does seem almost a pity, doesn't it? She's had her last hour of freedom."

"She's free right now, free as air. She'll always rest and play more than she'll work. You won't ride so much; she's lucky."

"I didn't mean that. I mean—now, she'll always have to come when you call. That isn't being free."

"Well—no—mebbe. But I wouldn't suppose you set such store by freedom." Steve, too, had heard about Damaris's intentions, her desire.

She stopped short and looked at him, seeing that he had applied what she had said to herself, taking it in, feeling that she must explain.

"I don't. There isn't such a thing, really. But I'm sorry for any wild creature when it comes time to learn that there are better things than freedom. It is better—isn't it?—to be safe and—and taken care of—to serve a master—than to be alone and wild. But," she twisted

her wrist, opened her hand as if to let something drop, "you do lose something, if you're a colt."

"Shall we let her go now? Not finish breaking her?" He watched Damaris, laughing, half teasing, but with loving eyes.

She shook her head. "It's too late. She's acquainted with fear now, so we must give her security." Then she laughed, too. "I *am* being silly, when I want to ride so much. There's nothing to do in Sunbury but play tennis. Do you play tennis?"

At that point the conversation ceased to have any interest for me. I went on past them, into the house. Cousin Clara was in the sitting room with Grandmother and Cousin Anne.

"Oh, there you are, Elizabeth," she said. "Is the circus over? We must be going; I've kept the horse standing long enough. You run tell Damaris, will you? . . ."

I went as bade to send Damaris in. Then from the corner of the house I watched Steve follow after her, observed his shy approach to Cousin Clara; I saw him, forgetful of the state of his hands, offer to help Damaris into the carriage. But she was up like a bird and over the wheel before he could touch her.

* * *

Soon Steve resolved that he would go to work f
Uncle Aaron on the farm. When Gran'pa took out t
horse and buggy one morning, to make his round
calls, Steve got in with him.

The farm was always quiet and peaceful and g
Like Uncle Aaron, and like what Steve wanted. I
pose it seemed good because the farm had been n

the fields sowed and harvested, by good men, always: by men who had been sober, kind, and quite simply and unostentatiously pious. And if Steve was perhaps not pious, still he belonged on the farm, because he had in him the same kind of goodness that had been his ancestors'.

I missed him in the days that followed, and yet it seemed to me right that he should be on the farm, a part of summer as I had always known it there, where he would feel at home, as in Heaven: where chicory bloomed among the orange lilies along the roadside, and Queen Anne's lace and purple thistles—where there would be forever that long view from the top of the hill by the house, through the barn, irresistibly drawing the eye: the faraway hill beyond the valley, and on that hill the single remote elm tree, black against the red disk of the setting sun. Summer there was eternal, yet it passed and altered: the first vivid universal green of Maytime paled in the grains and grasses, faded from hill and pasture through gold and russet to the color of straw, but in the trees gathered and deepened and darkened, until from a little way off, in the heavy shadows cast by the midsummer sun, it was not green at all, but indigo, where woods lay beyond the ripe fields.

* * *

One afternoon while I skated backward down a street in town, I brought up abruptly against a solid standing figure. "Whoa there, Susy!" Two strong hands on my shoulders steadied me, and faced me about.

"Hello! It's Elizabeth—"

I grinned up at Cousin John, unabashed. He

pinched my cheek and pulled my plait. He wasn't polite like Cousin Tune, but at least he had this gift, among others: no matter how many weeks might pass without his thinking of you, when you met he always made you feel that you were the one person in the world he most wanted to see.

Now his black eyes danced and sparkled. His tight collar, his trim little grizzled mustache made his jaw seem fuller, his red cheeks redder, his expression more jovial. He patted my shoulder with one hand, the other already in his trouser pocket, jingling its contents.

"How's your Gran'ma? How's the new Wild West cousin?"

"Oh—he's nice."

"That's what Damaris says." And he laughed, his deep, rich, hearty laughter that shook his comfortable body. "He's breakin' her filly for her to ride."

"I know; I was there. He's good with horses," I said, proudly.

"And she's teachin' him to play tennis."

Tennis! And I had thought him working on the farm!

"Nunnery, indeed!" Cousin John snorted, heartily. "Well, he's a good boy, I guess. Looks like his pop." Then he brought his hand out of his pocket. "Look-ye, Elizabeth: if I had time, I'd go in the drugstore and treat myself to a nectar soda with you, but I haven't, so you take this dime and have one without me, will you? And be sure to remind your Gran'ma, 'case I don't see her: we're lookin' for all of you on the Fourth. Steven, too. You won't forget?"

I reassured him, thanked him, and skated into the drugstore, my mind tumultuous with thoughts of the

Fourth at Cousin John's: giant crackers; lemonade; all the cousins from round about; fried chicken, watermelon; rockets, pinwheels, Roman candles.

When I had climbed to a stool at the soda fountain, my feet hanging heavy, weighted with the skates, a hand pulled aside the curtain in the door to the back room, and Cousin Tune came out. I was not particularly surprised to see him: that was where the town's idlers played their games of rum.

When Cousin Tune saw me, he had his hat off in a twinkling; he bowed, and stood with it in one hand, his cane swinging idly in the other.

"You haven't been to see us—Steve—for ages," I reproached him.

"No, I've been out of town. How is Steve?"

"He's fine. He's breaking a horse for Damaris."

"Ah—Romeo, Romeo!" He whistled between his teeth under his breath as he stood there watching me.

"Cousin John doesn't mind," I assured him, consolingly. "I just saw him, an' he particularly invited Steve for the Fourth. I bet he'd even give him a job someday, if he wanted one."

Surprise, displeasure showed for fleeting instants in Cousin Tune's face before it stiffened into a cold disdain.

"Steve isn't going to ask him. He'd get nowhere that way. A mill hand! No . . . If you see him, tell him I'm at the hotel; he's to come and see me. And give my regards to your grandmother, Elizabeth."

I accepted my chocolate soda from the fountain clerk and bent to the straw. I thought, "If one of them's mad, it's Cousin Tune, not Cousin John." That was odd; it was also, in a way, important. For what an uncle wanted and expected of a nephew might count for very little with the nephew; what a grandfather required of a granddaughter, on the other hand, might very likely be unquestioning obedience.

I was confused in my mind, and troubled. Whether I wanted it to happen or not, it sounded as if perhaps Steve had fallen in love with Damaris. I had hoped for it once, briefly, as one does hope for excitement in a sleepy summer, and now I felt guilty, as if my wishing had made it true. I could not forget the morning I had seen Damaris coming from church; I wished that I could show her, so, to Steve, so that he might understand. I was glad we had been asked to Uncle Aaron's for dinner that Sunday before the Fourth so that I might see for myself how he felt.

* * *

When we turned in Uncle Aaron's gate the next Sunday, and Ben lowered his head for the pull up the hill, dinner was ready and waiting for us. I looked for Steve in vain in the brief moment before we were led into the dining room. It was after we had gathered at the table that he came in; Uncle Aaron had waited for him before asking the blessing. I bent my head reverently enough, but lifted my eyes to look through my lashes at Steve. He was all dressed up, and he was dressed like the town boys, in white trousers and shirt and a bright tie. Perhaps it was the white shirt that made his face seem so dark and thin. It would never be a contented, quiet face like Uncle Aaron's—nor a jolly one like Cousin John's, nor an aristocratic one like his uncle Tune's—

but it was, I felt sure, a happy face. I sighed and forgot my unreasonable forebodings.

Uncle Aaron said "Amen," and we put our napkins in our laps as Cousin Anne started around with the plates of fried chicken. The men began to speak about the farm, and I knew at once that Steve liked it, liked being there. Most of the talk was of weather, cattle, and crops, but once Steve turned to Grandmother and said abruptly, "D'you know the ash tree that stands at the corner of the woods where the creek goes under the fence and through Welch's pasture? That's the ash the first surveyor marked when he laid down great-grandfather's bounds, the same tree—and that's been a hundred years and more."

Although I could not have put it into words, I knew what had kindled Steve's imagination: the same tree, the same boundary line, the same family, a hundred years. Land that because of long possession seemed sentient, living and loving like the very beasts, the cattle and horses. I thought, "Steve's found his house. He'll be here always." That carried me along to another conclusion, "Then he's not in love with Damaris," and I was comforted, for I knew that he would never think of Damaris and the Barkalow farm together.

But after dinner while I was still helping Grandmother and Cousin Anne with the dishes, Steve came to the kitchen door and bade us good-bye: Uncle Aaron had given him permission to use one of the horses, and he had hitched it to the buggy and was off for the afternoon.

I dared to say "Where's he going?" while I watched him drive down the slope past the kitchen window, but I knew it was useless before the words were uttered: that was the rudest question, almost, that a child could ask of any adult.

Grandmother said, "Tut! Reckon if Steve knows, that's all that's necessary." And Cousin Anne, "He's his own master. I wouldn't think of askin' him."

I felt forlorn and dismal: Steve had forgotten me. I said again, tentatively, "He had on tennis shoes."

"Oh, he'd hardly play tennis on *Sunday*. . . . He does go in, in the evenings sometimes, when they aren't workin' late in the fields."

I ceased to listen. I had learned what I wanted to know and I was all uncertain again, and troubled in spirit.

* * *

Fourth of July, in those early days of the century, was celebrated with gusto. For those who wanted them there were speeches on the courthouse lawn; there were picnics, there were family reunions, and a pervading feeling in the air of the more the merrier, both as to numbers and as to noise. But Cousin John was the only householder in town who had yard enough—all the way downhill to the creek—for the proper display of fireworks. Built I suppose in the '70s, his was still one of the newer big houses in town, and the grounds had never been divided to provide building sites for daughters and granddaughters.

On the morning of the Fourth, when Grandmother and I went up those steps, they were crowded with children and firecrackers. In the open double door, Cousin Clara and Cousin John were receiving their guests. When I had shaken hands with her and Cousin

John, and handed my hat with its wet, chewed elastic to Grandmother to dispose of, I followed the other children out to the curb, properly equipped with punk and firecrackers, cane-and-caps, and a box of torpedoes.

A quick glance into the parlor had sufficed to show me that all the cousins were there from all the farms around—and Uncle Aaron and Cousin Anne. Even Cousin Tune had come, and that I think had never happened before. Fourth of July was like Christmas: it took all one's attention to itself, particularly in the morning, when there was still an unexpended wealth of fireworks on hand. I had barely an eye to notice, while I sat in the gutter with my younger cousins, firing crackers, or stood on the carriage step, hurling torpedoes down on the sidewalk, that Steve and Damaris were playing tennis against some man I had never seen before. On the court Damaris came to life like a bird on the wing; Steve, so much slower, swung his racket awkwardly when a ball came his way, and waited, most times, for her to fly before him on light feet.

When we were called to dinner I heard the strange man's name; Mr. Leigh was introduced to one after another of the cousins, who said "Glad to know you," and didn't look glad at all. Cousin John explained him as "the manager of the Woodstock mill," but that was no justification of his presence at a family party, where there had never been strangers before. I resented his being there. He was a young man, but he didn't seem young to me then because he was so at ease and confident, so comfortable with all those country cousins: I resented him because he clearly belonged to another world—Cousin John and Cousin Clara's—which was so superior to all other worlds that its inhabitants could feel at home in any of them.

That should have been Damaris's world, too, but it wasn't. Particularly that day it wasn't, for then, if never again, she was in love with Steve with all her heart. Perhaps no one else noticed it, but I saw her eyes on him, proud and fond and unwithholding. She had emerged, for an hour at least, from behind her elusive wariness; she was loving and trustful. I was bewildered, but I was happy too when I looked at Steve and saw his happiness. An awkward, breathless happiness, almost frightened, as if he knew it was too good to be true. In company with him I held my breath.

I saw all this happen as we gathered in the dining room, and then I lost it because I was separated from them. And perhaps it was lost to them too, for always, in that very room. I never saw it again: not that faith and trust, that unreserve, in Damaris's eyes.

There must have been sixty people crowded that summer day into the immense dining room of the house on Hill Street. It was a room paneled in dark wood, with a parquet floor, with a heavy, elaborate sideboard built in at one end, and at the other, stained glass in a deep bay window. The children were put together at a low table set crosswise beneath those windows; the sun shining through them made blobs of color that were incongruous on the hearty country dinner that filled our plates. I know what we had to eat, not so much because I remember that particular day as because we always had it: fried chicken and mashed potatoes and gravy, tomatoes, peas, beans, biscuits, honey and jelly, pickled pears, pickled peaches, apple butter, tall glasses of lemonade, and, finally, thick crescents of watermelon.

"I'll bet," said Cousin John, with his usual hearty good nature, "I'll bet you never heard anything good about me in your life."

I stole a glance over my shoulder. He was leaning back in his chair, with his arm crooked over it and his napkin in his hand, swinging.

"I saved your father from disgrace, once. Saved his life, maybe. And 'twouldn't'a' been human nature if he'd ever forgiven me for it.

"It was in the winter of '65, or the spring—no, the winter, because it was shortly after we'd left Savannah—but we were out of South Carolina and into North—oh well—it don't matter. The war was nearly over, anyway. We'd gone all the way with Sherman, Condit and I, only he was in one division and I was in another—and somehow we'd never run across each other. Though I had seen Tune once, remember, Tune? In that hell'n'gone hullabaloo in Columbia?

"Well, it was after that I saw Cond. We were in North Carolina, marching through the woods. The pine woods, where they make turpentine. And they were on fire in spots.

"I had an orderly with me—I was ridin' to overtake my company, goodness knew where ahead of us. There was a cabin back amongst the trees—a log cabin—the only one around, and we could barely see that one for the smoke in those pine trees. We were past it when we heard an outcry and a woman screaming, and men's voices. So we left the road and went back to see. The door was open. There were four people in that one-room hut: A girl in the corner, crouched down, her long hair every which way, her frock torn off her shoulders, hiding behind Cond. He stood, back to her, with a bayonet in his gun. Facing Cond, getting ready to jump him, were two big bummers. He'd pricked one of 'em with his bayonet; he was holdin' his wrist to stop it bleedin'. Cond couldn't take his eyes off them, to look at us, but the girl—she couldn't'a' been more'n fifteen, sixteen—said, 'Oh, help him,' an' burst out cryin'.

"Well, the two ruffians didn't wait—when they saw the door blocked, they made for the window. There wasn't any glass in it. I let 'em go. They hadn't done anything, Cond had got there in time. I said, 'Howdy, Cond.' And he said, 'So it's you, John,' and he saluted. That made me kind o' mad—cousins like us who'd grown up together. An' he put a lot in that salute—kind o' mockin' the shoulder straps, an' the orderly, an' the horse an' all. Instead o' bein' grateful. He wasn't grateful, of course. He'd rather have spitted the villains on his bayonet. So I saluted back, and then I said something like 'The miscreants are fled: the damsel is saved. Will you return with us now to the column of march?' Damn silly of me, I know, bein' so smart—but Cond looked like the hero of a melodrama: face white and nostrils twitchin' an' breath comin' hard. All for a piney woods gal in a drab calico frock. It struck me funny. But he couldn't see it. He said, 'I'm stayin' right here. They may be back any minute.' He looked around at the girl, an' she stopped cryin' an' looked up at him. She was a rare-lookin' gal, I'll say that for her, and for Cond, too. I don't know—if she'd looked at me like that . . .

"But I said, 'Don't be a damn fool. The woods are on fire.' He said, 'I must get her to a place where she'll be safe.' I said, 'You'll never catch up with your regiment if you waste more time. They're ahead of us.'

Then—still bein' a damn fool myself—I went on when he didn't show signs of movin': 'Obey orders, Cond, and rejoin your regiment at once.'

"He tossed his gun into a corner of the room, bayonet an' all. He put his hands on his hips an' said, 'Be damned if I'll take orders from you, John Barkalow. Here I stay, until I can take her out with me. What the hell,' says Cond, 'this war's over, ain't it? There's no more rebels in this woods, anyway, only our own blankety-blank-blank bummers. I've fought for four years, an' if Sherman needed me I'd fight four more—but he don't, an' I'm quittin'.' "

Cousin John straightened around in his chair to face his audience squarely, and he brought his stubby old man's fist down on the table, and made the fork fall off the edge of the platter.

"D'you understand? Cond aimed to desert, then and there—an' stood up bold as brass an' told me so. Pretty small pun'kins, he must'a' thought I was—there wasn't much choice o' what I could do. I wouldn't arrest him, my own cousin. What would you have done?" He asked this of Steve quite seriously.

"Gone off an' left him, I reckon. What did you do?" The question came from the boy haltingly, reluctantly.

"Steve's being polite," I thought. "He doesn't want to hear this at all." I could feel him pushing the whole incident from him, tense with the effort.

"I stepped up to him as if I were going to argue, and before he saw it coming, I hit him on the chin and knocked him out. The girl was all over him in a second—she fought like a wildcat—but we finally got her off, and the orderly and I got Cond out and loaded him on my horse, and the girl on the orderly's—we had to take her, too, 'count o' the fire. We dropped her at the first crossroads store. That night I saw Cond to his own regiment—fifteen, twenty miles down the road—with some dispatch riders. Of course he'd come to just a few minutes after we had him on the horse. When we put the girl down Cond said to her, 'I'll be back.' That's all. He never spoke a word to me. He never did speak to me again; he never forgave me."

I turned to steal a glance at Steve, halfway down the table. He was leaning back in his chair, his chin on his chest, the wayward lock of hair in his eye. His sensitive face was stiff; it looked thin and drawn. He said, "No—I can see he wouldn't, you never gave him a chance to fight."

"No, young man, I didn't." Cousin John laughed. "I could have beaten him, I think, in a fair fight, but I'd'a' been marked sure, an' remember my orderly was there. Cond would'a' been in trouble aplenty for striking an officer. No, sir—up to that time the family'd come through the war without a black mark against us, an' I drew the line at desertion. Cond and I'd never hit it off an' I wouldn't'a' bothered if we hadn't been cousins. But I saved him from disgrace, an' maybe from bein' shot—an' he never forgave me. That's forty year ago, an' more, an' I never heard him speak a word after I hit him, an' never saw him again after I sent him off to his regiment. He fought to the end and marched in the Grand Review, and after his discharge, be damned if he didn't go back to North Carolina for that girl. He married her an' brought her home, and that didn't work out very well—she wasn't our kind of womenfolks, and just naturally hated Yankees besides. So he took her out to Texas."

"Then you mean—she wasn't a planter's daughter disguised?" Damaris's voice was high, tremolo, falsely light. She looked carefully away from Steve toward her grandfather. "I don't like the end of your story," she complained.

"I know," Cousin John chuckled. "You wouldn't. You read too many highfalutin novels. Every girl 't grew up in Georgia or the Carolinas, in the sixties, lived in a mansion that got burned by Sherman's soldiers. But there weren't any planters in those piney woods." Then he saw Steve's face. He added hurriedly, "I reckon Cond made her out something extra-special. We all do the girls we marry."

"Anyway," said Damaris, "anyway"—her voice was firmer, two spots of color burned in her cheeks—"she had courage. Think of it: to leave everything—home—behind her, and marry a Yankee soldier she scarcely knew."

"Pshaw—she didn't stand to lose anything. What'd she have? I always wondered how Cond made out in Texas, but when I've been in those parts never had the courage to go and see. I don't like having doors shut in my face."

"Oh, Gran'pa! As if anyone'd dare!" Damaris reached across the corner of the table between them and tweaked his ear. "But just the same, you were horrid to Cousin Cond. Sherman didn't need him, did he? And how was he to know what would happen to his girl? Steve has told me all about her: how she wouldn't talk about the War because she was still a rebel, but how lovely she was and how good."

"You see," said Steve slowly, "I never knew Mom 'n' Pop when they were young. Mom must'a' been nigh forty when I was born, and she died when I was nine. She wasn't—pretty—I know, really—then. I only thought she was, because she was so good to me. All the prettiness 'd been worked out of her, long before. But there was a daguerreotype taken just after they were married. . . . I made up all that about her bein' a planter's daughter, because I thought she must'a' been. She looked so—I dunno—fierce an' sweet—an' gallant." He blushed over his own adjectives but he got them out.

"You mean to say," Cousin John demanded, "that you never knew how they met?" Steve shook his head. "I've got Pop's discharge papers, and his corps badge, put away, but he never talked much about the War.

"It was so long ago, now," Steve said bravely, "I can't see any of it matters much. Poor Pop—he never knew how to make a go of things. That was the War, maybe. There's lots like him—Cousin Tobias Van Doren . . ." He was talking at random, in a valiant effort to distract attention from himself, his people, his background. "Cousin Tobe, now—was he with you in Georgia an' all?"

Cousin John only snorted. Cousin Tune said, shortly, "He was wounded at Chickamauga. He never fought after that."

Cousin Clara put an end to the situation. She rose from her chair at the end of the table, and everyone followed her example. I had heard all that was going to be heard, obviously; I went out to find the others of my age, to help set off the remaining firecrackers and to wait, with exquisite anticipation, for the big fireworks display.

* * *

Steve was on the farm after the Fourth, waiting for the wheat to dry so that the threshing could begin. I felt as if I had had a story snatched away from me half-read; with Steve away I could have no idea of what advances were made, what complications ensued. It was something of a comfort to me to reflect that Steve would have no time for tennis lessons at Cousin John's, nor even, probably, for horseback riding at Uncle Aaron's.

I had seen the beginning, the first chapter of a romance; I knew that, because on the Fourth of July I had seen how Damaris looked at Steve. Nothing had been said for a long while about her desire to enter a convent. I hoped she had forgotten it, but if she hadn't, Cousin John was impossible of resistance. I realized that after I heard him tell how he had carried Cousin Cond back to the army and his duty. I hoped that his plans for Damaris stopped with keeping her out of the convent.

Mr. Leigh was far too much in Sunbury: all his Sundays were spent at the Barkalows'. He came to church with Cousin Clara and Cousin John, but it was Damaris he came to see, not they. Grandmother said to Gran'pa when we got home from church that John had found his substitute for the convent.

I was sure that Damaris loved Steve, and I told myself that Cousin John couldn't be cruel, yet I was glad Steve was on the farm. I was obscurely apprehensive lest he need to measure himself against the other man, who was so secure, so safe from any uncertainty of himself or his world.

Chapter Four

Summer advanced slowly. Queen Anne's lace spread across the pastures and in every waste place; the tousle-headed wild bergamot bloomed in clumps beside the road, at the edges of the woods, and in the ditches, and even if you didn't see it, the thick fragrance came sharp to the nostril. There was still chicory, pale in the meadows, and here and there the brilliant burnt orange of the butterfly weed. In every country garden there was bergamot, too—the scarlet bergamot that smells like barbers' bottles—and orange and yellow day lilies, and magenta phlox. In Grandmother's yard were petunias and verbenas and marigolds—all the strong-colored flowers of midsummer.

One afternoon while Steve was still on the farm, I was at home alone. Cousin Bias came into the yard, swinging his bad leg painfully. He asked meekly if he might use Grandmother's spade for a while; he wouldn't bother me—he knew where it hung in the barn, and no one would mind.

I was frightened. I sat up, put my feet on the ground that I might feel less helpless, and said, "But Grandmother doesn't want the yard spaded up."

He twisted his cap in his gnarled yellow hands, and shifted his weight so that one shoulder sagged. "I'm at Mrs. Stuart's."

I knew Mrs. Stuart. She wouldn't want holes dug in her yard either.

"Did she send for the spade?"

He looked stubbornly at the ground. His cap went round and round in his hands.

"She didn't, did she? There isn't any buried treasure there; she'd have found it long ago."

He didn't look angry, only troubled. His tight little square face was very sad, his eyes pleading. "I've got to look everywhere. I can't remember where I buried it."

"Oh, you . . . you buried it yourself?" This I had not heard about his mania. Bias had this idea he was going to find buried treasure someplace. Grandmother had told him to stop his "foolishness"—that no one was going to give him work if he went on making holes on their property. I had thought it was bandit's gold, or miser's gold, he was looking for. It was more incredibly fantastic that he should believe he had ever had gold to bury.

"Yes, I buried it myself. D'you think I'm a robber?" He muttered a few unintelligible words, then in a sharper, more insistent tone, argued with me, "And I've got to dig everywhere, because I've forgotten—I need it, I tell you. I gotta keep that girl of mine off the streets."

I knew his "girl," Virgie Van Doren, although I should never have called her so. It made me a little sick to think she was a cousin of Steve's. She was an awkward, draggle-tailed woman with an unwashed-looking sallow skin, lank black hair, and gloomy, defiant eyes. I knew their house, too, and her squalid, fly-bitten little grocery store.

I did not want to know what Bias meant; I said sullenly, "She's not on the street. She's got a grocery store."

He blinked at me, then began to nod his head.

"That's so. I forgot how time passes. She's got a store now. But she's got a boy to be schooled, too. God, I need that gold—if I could only think—" He rubbed his forehead with a stiff rheumatic hand.

"Where'd you get the gold?" I was too astonished not to ask him that, but I was immediately sorry, and frightened again, because his mouth twisted so, his eyes glared so furiously. I said it quickly. "I know it's none of my business."

"'S all right," he laughed. "I got it—but it's not for you to hear. I got it all right. Not where the others got theirs—Tune, an' John Barkalow, an' your Gran'pop, an' them. Oh, I know—I know how come they're all so rich. Gold an' silver they dug up in Georgy where 'twas hid, an' brung back with 'em. But I never got to Georgy. The damn bastards got me at Chickamauga."

Somewhere I had heard madmen must be humored. I drew a long breath, and exclaimed in a shaken voice, "Chickamauga! I never knew till lately you were there. I always wanted to find someone—to hear about it. All I hear is Sherman. I want to know about General Thomas. 'The Rock of Chickamauga,' they call him in the history. Were you one of his men?"

I wasn't so precociously diplomatic as this may seem: I knew well how veterans loved to describe their battles.

"Hap Thomas. Yes, I was in his command at Chickamauga." He put one hand on the trunk of the apple tree, and leaned his weight on it. He smiled; his face was gentle and quite sane. "The others broke and ran. We didn't run, not with him there."

Bias was still telling me about Chickamauga when Grandmother came in. Grandmother went directly from the front gate to the front door, without seeing him, but Bias scrambled to his feet, said good-bye rather hastily, and slipped back into the alley the way he had come.

Chapter Five

We were in the heat of summer then. Days were long, heavy, somnolent; locusts sang in all the trees, a stupefying chorus. It was too hot to do anything but read, or swing lazily in the hammock without reading.

I looked for locust shells on the tree trunks and collected them. The heat made one childish; I lay on the grass with them spread before me and they became a herd of buffalo crossing the plains, or elephants in a circus procession, or race horses to be stabled in the hollows between and under the upthrust roots of the apple tree. I thought much of Steve and Damaris, but days passed and I saw neither of them, and so could not look on at their wooing.

Steve came back to Grandmother's when the threshing was done. Uncle Aaron had no need, for a while, of an extra hand, but he would have kept him on, Steve told me.

"Where would it ever get me, though?" he asked. He sounded almost savagely resolute. "I've got to get ahead in a hurry. Like that Mr. Leigh. I've been one o' those no-good Van Dorens long enough."

"Oh, Steve! You aren't!" I protested angrily. "Besides, I thought you wanted to write poetry."

"Poetry?" He hesitated. "Poetry! D'you reckon I could ever earn a living that way? I know the farm is where I belong. But it won't—" and he repeated it stubbornly, "it won't get me anywhere."

And so he went job hunting again. Loyalty or pride or timidity kept him from applying to Cousin John. He went the rounds, from store to store, from livery stable to grain elevator to lumber and coal yard.

One evening at dinner Gran'pa, who was the local doctor for the railroad, told us that a freight yard laborer had strained his back. Steve might get a start there while the injured man was laid off.

Grandmother didn't like it. Once, only the Irish had been good enough for the railroads, and that was as it should be. No Barkalow had ever done that kind of work, nor, if she had her say, ever would.

Steve laughed at her. "Don't forget," he said, "I don't look to find my money: I aim to earn it."

Perhaps through Gran'pa, he was taken on at the freight depot, in the injured man's place, with no assurance the job would last more than a week. He was put to work at once loading and unloading cars.

Grandmother had too much respect for his independence to scold him, but I heard her say to Gran'pa one night, "I should think you had better sense. The boy's not fit for work like that: he'll mash a foot or maim himself some way."

"Nonsense, Libby." Gran'pa sounded amused. "D'you think it's harder work than loading wheat?"

"He's not used to it. He don't know enough to be careful. I'm scared the railroad'll be the death of him."

In that summer, when Steve worked at the freight depot for a little while, whenever I could I stepped across the bridge through the bottoms, over the trestle, to the freight office door, to see if I could catch sight of him. For that brief while I felt myself on a different footing with the station workers and with the engineers whom

I knew to wave to: I was no longer merely one of the traveling public; I was connected with the railroad.

Sometimes I managed to be there in midafternoon, and on one Friday afternoon, when I was sitting in the torrid sun on the edge of an empty baggage truck, swinging my heels, Damaris drove the Barkalow carriage up the hill. She came to a stop beside me, but she did not look once toward the freight depot. She showed no surprise at finding me there, but her cheeks were flushed and her voice breathless when she spoke.

"Hello, 'Liz'beth," she said. "Are you meeting this train, too?"

"Oh no, just watching." I stopped swinging my heels.

"Gran'ma sent me. Gran'pa's on it, and I guess he's bringing Mr. Leigh. For over Sunday."

She embraced Cousin John when he appeared, fanning himself with his hat, but she greeted Mr. Leigh with a languid and indifferent hand. I had decided that I should not tell Steve that Damaris had been there to meet Mr. Leigh: even if he knew she had been sent by Cousin Clara, he might be troubled.

The freight yard was a brief episode in the summer. The injured laborer came back; there was no longer a place for Steve. He had hoped that his first job would lead to something else, but the money he had been paid was all he had to show for it. He came back downhearted to spend his days with me, or working in the yard for Grandmother.

But downhearted or not, he went to spend his evenings at the Barkalows'. He had decided, he told me, that he might as well not look for steady work until after haying time at Uncle Aaron's.

At haying time, meadows were snowed under with Queen Anne's lace, chicory was fading. The crushed-raspberry heads of joe-pye weed were lifted high above the thickets to make their spectacular annual show. The spears of the blue vervain bloomed beside the fences, and all the air was sweet again with clover. Haying time was a lovely time on the farm. Steve would want to stay there forever and ever, once he had raked the sweet-smelling alfalfa. I hoped that Uncle Aaron would understand that, and give it to him to do.

The weather was hot. Steve dozed in the hammock, a handkerchief over his face, while I played in the grass with the locust shells. He was lazy; he was also quiet and at peace.

It must have been during that interval of time when nothing happened—when it seemed as if nothing would ever happen—that Steve and I spent a Sunday afternoon walking in the cemetery. Or perhaps it was earlier: before he went to work at the freight depot, or while he was there. The date is unimportant; I can only be sure that it was after that afternoon when I had talked to Bias, and he had put ideas into my head that I would not take out and look at, like the implied cause-and-effect connection between lack of money and being "on the street."

It was generally for want of something better to do that you walked in the cemetery, but so many Sunday afternoons in my life had been empty of anything at all to do that the cemetery had long since become familiar to me, and unfrightening.

On the afternoon when Steve and I went to walk there, the sun was still shining overhead. We wandered at random along the paths, Steve watching idly for any stones marked Van Doren, occasionally stopping to lay his hand on a tree trunk, or crossing the grass to an old-fashioned aboveground sarcophagus, to rub at the lichened, eroded letters and try to make them legible. One of these I remember was broken: a triangular piece was gone from one end, down near the ground, and I wondered whether if you knelt and peered in, you might possibly see white bones in the dark. I had no inclination to try it, but with Steve there beside me, so quiet but so content, so acquiescent and unrebellious, I did not shrink from dwelling on the horrors that suggested themselves to me: such horrors as peeking into a tomb at a moldering skeleton.

But when the sun slipped down the sky before we noticed, other stray pedestrians disappeared from those green aisles, and far away at the top of the hill above the railroad tracks, two figures came clambering up between the trees. At that distance they were nothing—could be nothing—but a blurred suggestion of man and woman, but for some reason—suddenly, out of my submerged memories of what Bias had said to me that afternoon at Grandmother's—there rose and flooded over me, making my heart beat thick and fast, the conviction that the woman might be Virgie Van Doren. I leaned sideways against Steve, and took his arm in both my hands.

"Let's go now, Steve. They close the gates at sunset."

I suppose my voice was queer. He stared at me. "You're all tired out, 'Liz'beth. I never meant to walk you too far."

"You didn't. It's just—let's go before they shut the gates."

No doubt he thought I was afraid of the cemetery

in the twilight. He did not see the woman. After that first glimpse, after I had turned my back, I did not see her myself. As soon as we were outside the gate, walking down the avenue, I knew how silly I had been: there had been nothing in the world about that woman—nothing individual or recognizable—to suggest a name, a face, a figure that I knew.

The memory I have of that afternoon is of an occasion too trivial to make it important that I should date it more certainly than I have: It was after I talked to Bias; it was before the evening when Virgie Van Doren came to our house to see Gran'pa. And that must have been on a Sunday, too; otherwise Gran'pa would not have been at home. I suppose that on other evenings Virgie kept her little grocery open.

Virgie's visit, and all that followed, brought the summer quickly to its dramatic climax. Grandmother had gone to church. Gran'pa was on the front porch, rocking and smoking his pipe; we could hear his rockers creak. Steve and I were around the house between the end of the porch and the sitting room window. With twigs—thin twigs I had broken from the syringa bush and stripped of leaves—Steve was building a Texas ranch for me. Pop-eyed locust shells were cattle and horses; patiently, with steady fingers and a surprisingly delicate touch, Steve made a corral for them, one twig on another twig.

When the gate squeaked, we scarcely looked up; we couldn't see, around the corner of the house, who was coming. I heard Gran'pa knock out his pipe on the porch rail.

"Well, Virgie. You want to see me?" He opened the screen door for her and they went into the house. Then after a moment, I heard her strident voice inside. The sitting room window was open.

"But I tell you, Doctor, he's gone crazy, diggin' for gold. Ain't there nothing I can do?"

I think Steve did not even pay attention at first. He was intent on the task he had set himself: the twigs were tiny and frail in his big hands, and as he laid them in place he held his breath. I could watch him and listen, too, and I felt no compunction about listening; it was certainly no secret that Bias was crazy.

I couldn't understand what Gran'pa answered; his deep voice was a mumble-bumble well withdrawn from the window. Virgie said, "I never thought no medicine would help. But you're a doctor—you can tell me what to do. If he dug up that thousand dollars he's lookin' for—dug it up some'eres it was put for him to find—would he be satisfied?"

I did hear Gran'pa then: he murmured something noncommittal about not ministering to a mind diseased, and then objected. "You haven't got a thousand dollars, anyway." Gran'pa was inclined to bluntness with his patients.

"The old man don't see good anymore." Her heavy voice was almost eager. "If I filled a cigar box with new pennies, d'you think he'd see they weren't gold pieces?"

"They weigh different."

"I don't believe he could tell, his hands are so bad with rheumatics."

"And if he tried to spend 'em—"

"He wouldn't. He'd give 'em to Charley. He's set his heart on school for him. That's why he's diggin' everywheres in such a hurry. Charley's fifteen."

"Why a thousand dollars, anyway? He never had a

thousand dollars, all at one time, in his life."

"Oh yes he did. You wouldn't know about that, would you? That was a secret." Virgie's tone was concentrated bitterness, ugliness—the ugliness of lees in the bottom of a cup long cold. "Rich men don't care how many people know one grandchild costs 'em a fortune, but they're mighty careful not to let it out 'at another one cost 'em a thousand. . . . Sure, Pop had a thousand to keep his mouth shut, an' mine, an' he never made no trouble, neither did I. But she found out about it, just the same, and raised hell." Virgie repeated, "Raised hell, all right," with a triumphant satisfaction.

Steve had got to his feet, trampling corral and locust shells as he rose. He seized me by the elbows, lifted me up, and before I knew what was happening, he had me around the house on the summer kitchen steps.

"Lordy," he said, "we shouldn't ought to 'a' stayed where we could hear. But how'd we know it was going to be secrets? You forget what she said in there, d'you hear?"

"It doesn't matter whether I do or not," I confessed sadly. "I don't know what she was talking about."

"Me neither," he hastened to say. "At least, not *who.* So I reckon it's all right. Tell me about her, 'Liz'beth. . . . Poor old Bias—never had a chance."

"He was a soldier."

"And got wounded. There weren't any Barkalows had that rotten luck, you bet."

"No-o," I said doubtfully. "Some of them were killed. What I meant was: he must have some money, a pension. And Virgie has a grocery store, and Charley has a paper route."

"Oh—that black-eyed scowlin' kid that passes the

paper? I know him, then." Steve leaned back, his elbow on the step above the one where we sat. "It's funny, 'Liz'beth, but it's true: I'm every bit as much relation to that kid as I am to you. It don't seem right, somehow."

He sat up, put his elbows on his knees and ran his fingers through his hair, pressed his palms against his temples.

"Lea' me think a minute. . . . That's real trouble, 'Liz'beth: craziness loose in the house . . . D'you reckon if he did find his gold—? I got some money, now—what I earned at Uncle Aaron's, an' at the freight yard, besides a little Uncle Tune gi' me. I ain't aimin' to spend it, just now. I could send her some to put in her cigar box—real gold pieces. . . . Look, 'Liz'beth—you run up to bed now, an' don't say a word to anybody. I'll catch up with her when she goes, and suggest it. I can kind o' lead up to it, by way o' Bias's diggin' up Cousin Libby's yard, so she won't know we listened."

I didn't see Steve the next morning. In the evening I failed to catch him alone. It was the middle of the week before I knew he had lent Virgie a hundred dollars—all he had, all he'd earned—to put in a box for her father to dig up. After that, both of us waited to hear what happened—waited impatiently, but in vain.

On Saturday afternoon, when I was ready to go to the library and had got as far as the gate, Grandmother called after me from the porch to go tell Bias, or leave word for him, that the brick path needed weeding. I started back toward the steps, to protest; she stopped the words on my lips: she couldn't bear to cast him off completely, she would just have to lock the spade up and keep an eye on him. I decided to go willingly. I wanted to know how Virgie's experiment had turned out:

whether they had buried the money, whether he had found it, whether he believed. . . .

Steve would be curious, too—and Steve wouldn't be afraid of Bias. I wouldn't go looking for him but if I met him uptown, or saw him on my way to the library, I would ask him to go with me. And I did find him, in the drugstore. Damaris was beside him at the soda fountain counter, but that did not prevent my going in.

"Steve," I said, "I've got to go down to Bias's for Grandmother. Won't you go with me? I'm scared, kind of. . . ."

"Reckon we might as well. D'you mind?" he asked Damaris. He drained his soda noisily through the straw, got down from his stool, and helped Damaris to alight from hers. "We were going to take a walk, anyway, an' that's as good a direction as any."

As the three of us strolled down Main Street toward the West End he explained to Damaris:

"I had this hundred dollars I don't need right now. I got twenty gold pieces at the bank, for her to put in the box on top of her pennies. She thinks he won't know the difference."

"But, Steven—you'll never get it back, from people like that."

"Reckon I will, but if I don't," Steve said cheerfully, "I can make out. They're cousins of mine, down on their luck."

Bias's house was on a corner of two of the crooked streets in the West End; it was a drunken, unpainted, ramshackle old place, with the one-room grocery store tied to it, between house and pavement, by a series of roofs slanting crazily, covered with rusted tin. Steve went inside and leaned over a counter, dimly visible to us where we stood silent in the blazing sun. When he returned he told us Bias hadn't found the money yet.

"It's buried at the end of the pump trough, where the water runs, to make it look like it's been there a long while."

We went on up the path beside the house. There was a wide yard full of green bushes, and trees, but there was no grass. Every square foot of earth had been dug up, turned over, trampled down, until it looked like a raw lot where a new house is going up, and workmen walk on boards pushing wheelbarrows.

Only Charley was there, sitting on the edge of a tipsy, morning glory–covered side porch; he was bent over lacing up his shoes. When he heard us he lifted his shock of black hair to stare without a word; his feet as he moved them made a rasping noise in the gravel.

"I've got a message for your grandfather." I was disappointed, yet relieved too. I wasn't afraid of Charley. "Grandmother wants him Monday morning."

Then Bias came around the side of the house, dragging his spade.

Steve, with all a boy's impatience, took matters into his own hands. "Howdy, Cousin Tobias. Still diggin'? An' no luck? Looks to me there's only one place you haven't tried." He nodded toward the pump.

Bias frowned. "I couldn't'a' put it there, in the wet. Or did I? Gold won't rust." He brushed his awkward open hand down over his face. "I can't remember . . . might's well look, though. Easy diggin', that is."

He lurched down the path. The spade made a hideous sound dragging across the gravel behind him.

My heart stopped still. I held my breath. We all stood motionless where we were.

Bias turned over the sod, with its tufts of grass, then dug up one spadeful of damp, dark clay, and another. And the spade struck the box.

"There's somethin', Charley!" he called back, over his shoulder. His voice broke. "But I can't believe—it couldn't be my money, here." The denial was made as a shield against disappointment. He did believe: a dreadful joy in his voice broke through the words, belied them.

Slowly, shaking with excitement, he got down on his knees and looked. Then, wild-eyed, he brushed the dirt away, pulled the box out with both hands, and laid it on the ground.

Steve and I were already at his shoulder. Charley came running down the path. Damaris stood still by the porch.

With his thumbnail, Bias forced the lid open, threw it back.

"It is! It's my money! I found it, Charley—"

He plunged one hand into the box, seized a handful of coins, let them dribble through his fingers. They all looked alike, I thought, with a sick sense of relief, and if you didn't see well, anyway . . . The pennies were bright as the gold, mint-new, glittering in the sun as they spun and dropped.

But they didn't feel alike. Gran'pa had been right. Even in Bias's callused, swollen hands, gold was heavier than copper. His face changed; he panted; I thought he was going to faint. Instead he caught his breath, set his jaw, chose two coins and weighed them against each other. He tossed them aside and pawed through the box. Pennies tumbled over the edges, dropped in the mud. He looked up, past Steve and me, at Charley.

"You found it. God—you stole it. Thought you could fool me with coppers. It made a thief of you. My only grandson. A thief—" His voice dropped to a whisper. His pale eyes were wide, set in his wrinkled putty-colored face. He squatted there, as if he had been too shocked and too frightened to move. He held his fingers over the box and shook them, as if to drain off any pollution clinging to them.

"The filthy, dirty, stinkin' stuff—"

Then suddenly he made up his mind, and began fumbling in the mud for the spilled coins. When he had replaced them, he tucked the box under his arm, struggled to his feet, nodded his head wisely and gravely, and said, "I'll just put you where you can't do no more harm."

He limped back along the path that led to the outhouse and woodshed and chicken coop. We stood turned to stone; when we saw his intention we were too far away to stop him. He flung open the privy door and with one swing of his arm tossed away the box and its contents. We could hear the coins clash against each other as they dropped.

He closed the door again, returned without a word or even a glance at us, and went into the house by the kitchen door.

Damaris had come up beside me. She leaned on my shoulder, saying, "Steve—oh, Steve—"

"Don't take on about it. It don't matter to me—"

Charley turned to face him, head up, nostrils quivering. "To you! Why should it? 'Tain't you that's a thief—"

"I'm sorry. I've harmed you without meaning to. Can't you explain?"

"To him?"

"No—I know. Poor ol' coot. The money don't matter, I meant."

"That's right—the gold was yours—" It is hard to believe, now, that a boy's voice could ever have been so bitter. "You can try to get it back if you want to."

"I'd have to want it worse'n I do." Steve laughed shortly. "Keep it, an' welcome."

The boy's fists clenched, tears glittered in his black eyes, his face was white with fury. For a second he could not speak, then he burst out, "Jeez—you wait. Someday I'll have money enough to throw in all your faces. Then you'll see—"

"Hey, there—listen! I was only tryin' to help, like kinfolks ought—"

"Kinfolks!" Charley spat out the word, turned and leaped for the porch steps; he went inside and slammed the screen behind him.

We went away then, and took the opposite direction so as to avoid the grocery windows. Damaris was white and shivery. I felt sick, and without bones in my knees; I wanted to hold on to the fence as I walked, but I didn't.

Steve said, with his hand at Damaris's elbow, "I oughtn't to've taken you. I knew he was crazy. But he's harmless crazy. An' who knows: maybe we've cured him, anyway; surely he won't go diggin' anymore."

Steve's untroubled acceptance of the incident had its effect on me. By the time we had crossed the railroad tracks and were on Main Street again, the strength had come back to my knees, the sickness under my belt had subsided.

Damaris was still pale; she walked listlessly and

apart from Steve. I watched her, and hoped with all my heart that she would not always, from now on, when she was with him remember Bias and this afternoon.

Sometimes I was beside them, sometimes ahead, and sometimes I lagged behind, but I heard the few remarks they made on all the long way back uptown.

"Steven, when you were a little boy, you believed in fairy tales, didn't you? In the end, everything must come right: everyone must live happily, forever and ever."

"I'd like them to," Steve said, smiling down at her. "Why not?"

Damaris did not trouble to answer this question. "It makes you so—reckless—believing in fairy tales." She caught her breath. "I suppose that was all the money you've made, all summer. And now it's gone."

"I can earn more, once I find a job. I was hangin' on to enough to take me back to Texas. But if you—if I—if I have to go back, I reckon I can ride the rods."

"Oh, Steve—don't talk like that. You frighten me."

"'Tain't nothing to be frightened of. There's tramps on every train comes into the yards."

"I didn't mean that. I mean . . . don't think anyone wants you to go away. We like your being here, don't we, Elizabeth?"

I said, "Yes," and dropped my stick, and went and took Steve's hand in both my own, and looked up at him, troubled.

What I saw in his face made me catch my breath. He was too happy. And I understood so clearly what Damaris had meant: "Let's stay like this. . . . Let's not change at all. . . . Let this summer last." And Steve—blindly, betrayingly—misunderstood her.

It wasn't that I thought she didn't love him. But I believed she was denying it to herself, because she had wanted to be a nun. And would deny it to him, if he asked her.

On that day when we walked home from Bias's, I thought Damaris was wishing that the two of them could go on like that forever, that time would stand still. But I knew it was too late for such a wish—knew it while I was parting from them, and Steve was solemnly swearing me not to tell Grandmother a word about the afternoon, while Damaris was teasing him: "So you do know how foolish you've been, if you don't want Cousin Libby to know!" He was too happy with what she had said before to mind the teasing: she had made him so happy I could hardly bear to see it, and I went away from them wishing desperately that he wouldn't—that he *wouldn't* tell her how much he loved her. Because that would be the end of everything.

And that night came soon enough. Too soon. But before then Steve and I had the morning together that I have always remembered, up in the top of Grandmother's apple tree.

She had decided the tree was overloaded with fruit. If Steve and I would gather some of the green apples, those left on the boughs would ripen better. The culls need not be wasted: they would do for jelly. I liked Grandmother's apple jelly, clear and sweet and honey-colored.

Besides, I liked to climb the apple tree. Being lighter, I went high above Steve's head, and from the treetop surveyed the world around and below me.

"It's nice up here," I said, complacently. "Aren't you glad you're not in that hot old freight depot?"

"It's nice up here, sure. But unless I can pay my way I can't stay."

"Why not? Grandmother likes having you. Anyway, you can go back to the farm."

"Yes, and be a hired man. It's not what I want, exactly."

"Uncle Aaron worked for his father, and then when his father died, he got the farm."

"Don't, 'Liz'beth. 'Tain't right to think o' such things."

I had given up all pretense of working, and sat swinging in a kind of saddle where several branches united, and looked down through the leaves to the top of Steve's head. I couldn't see his face.

"But don't you want to stay, Steve?"

"I'm going to stay. It's home." He came a little higher and stood with his hand clasped around the trunk behind my feet, his face on a level with my knees. "When you've been away from here once, and come back," he went on, "you'll know what it's really like. Why—I wouldn't mind dying, even, if I knew I was here out there on the hill with the other Van Dorens. Not if I was buried where the rain would wash the smell of leaves and the roots of trees, tricklin' down through the grave clods."

"Steve!" I shrank away from him against the bough behind me. I could feel how small and choked my voice was. No one I knew talked about the grave—his own grave—in that casual, acquiescent fashion. Death sometimes, yes: "When I'm gone," but that meant "When I'm not here, when I'm in Heaven." I said, "How can you say such things?" Then I remembered that after all, Steve was a poet—after a fashion—and entitled to all a poet's strangeness.

I saw Damaris at our gate. She might have missed seeing me in the apple tree, but Steve was too big to be hidden by leaves and boughs, however thick. Beneath us, looking up, holding the brim of her hat to her cheeks with both hands, she said, "Whatever are you doing, perched up there?" Her face was bright and vivid, her eyes eager.

"We're supposed to be picking apples, but we're really just talking. Steve's been telling me where he wants to be buried."

"Oh, Steven!—shame—" She laughed at him, her voice soft and sweet. "Don't let him frighten you, Elizabeth. No one ever talks about his grave except when he doesn't really believe in it."

Steve was on the ground beside her by that time. I followed, but when, oblivious to me, they sat down together in the hammock, and Steve took up the volume of ballads he had left lying there, I turned my back on them and began to gather up the apples that were on the ground.

Damaris was happy; she could not be so, in his presence, unless she loved him. The skirtful of apples I had picked up fell tunk-tunking into the bucket. My mind sang "It's all right, after all. Everything's all right." I selected the largest, least worm-eaten apple to eat with a lump of salt in the kitchen, and left them in the hammock.

I had known, for a moment, the real Damaris, released and light of heart. I was never to see her again like that.

* * *

Before that morning, and after it, however happy I might be while the sun shone, my nights were troubled with bad dreams. I was haunted by fantastically confused images of Bias and Steve, and a Charley Van Doren who was Cousin John Barkalow when he was a boy in uniform. One night when I woke shivering cold with an inexplicable sense of horror, I lay for a moment thinking of that strange transformation—and then I understood. All the things I knew in the dark, secret places of my mind came together on the surface and were clear as a printed page.

Charley Van Doren looked like Cousin John: eyes, brow, the shape of his head; Cousin John was the rich man Virgie had meant, talking to Gran'pa. The rich man with two grandchildren. Virgie was "that woman" who brought on Ralph's divorce. And Damaris's mother—was the woman who had "raised hell." And left.

The horror that shook me then was a child's horror, partly helpless revolt, partly fear, partly vain desire to go back and not know. It was unfathomable.

I decided I must face it alone, must never say a word to anyone. Steve didn't know, or he would not have taken Damaris there. Damaris didn't know, or she wouldn't have gone. And Grandmother must never suspect my knowledge: you couldn't let a grown-up see how you had slipped under the surface they kept, glazed and hard, over dreadful possibilities: they might say, to comfort you, "Oh, well, life is like that"—when you wanted desperately not to find out, not yet, that life was like that.

With a kind of desperate revulsion I turned away from the grown-up world and went back to the ordinary summertime games of Sunbury boys and girls.

Chapter Six

As I write this, it is August again, and farmers are cutting their hay. In the thickets the joe-pye weed is fading; in the pastures the Queen Anne's lace is covered with dust. But goldenrod is yellow on the hills, and ironweed is coming into flower; fall thistles are in bloom by roadside fences, a mass of lavender.

That other summer must have been like this—abandoned, imperially splendid, with something premonitory in its splendor: the season for the last time wearing regality like a garment, all purple and gold. But to see in the magnificence of August a forewarning of the end is an inclination of the middle-aged mind. It is I now remembering who can see the August fields in a somber light.

The time has come when I must write of the end of summer, if I am to finish this at all. But I draw back from it, and hesitate, and linger on the thought of the Fourth of July, and the long, comparatively peaceful month that followed.

One of our childish amusements that year was to go forth at dusk armed with a snake made of a long black stocking, stuffed to the right thickness and attached to a long piece of string. In some vacant lot we put the snake down among the weeds, and carried the string to the other side of the street, where we concealed ourselves behind trees or a fence. When anyone—usually a pair of lovers, arm in arm—passed along beside the vacant lot, we pulled the string. The snake darted across their path, the girl screamed and lifted up her ruffled petticoats, and her cavalier pursued the stocking with a club or threw stones from a safe distance.

If a stray couple who cared more for the kind obscuring shadow than for light on their path came down the hill on the side of the street where we lay hidden, then we kept immovable and silent, our presence unsuspected. One night, a boy and girl stopped by the culvert railing to look down through black dark toward the stream. The willow tree, which like a tent covered us lying prone on the moss beneath it, was not fifteen feet from them, but they could not possibly see us. Neither could we recognize, in the dark, who they were. We could tell that they were arm in arm: the girl had on a light frock, the boy a dark coat. We could not withdraw without betraying ourselves, and we made no attempt to do so. We crossed our arms and laid our cheeks upon them, to wait in comfort, as we had done other times. I do not remember that I was conscious of shame until the girl spoke. I felt it then only because I knew the voice, and it was Damaris's.

"Please, Steve," she said, "please don't. Don't say it."

"Tell me this, then," and his voice was confident, almost teasing. "Do you still want to be a nun?"

I lifted my head. The two figures were a dim blur, outlined vaguely by the light beyond the trees, obscured by the leaves before my face. But I could see how close they stood, side by side.

Damaris said, in a quiet, resigned tone, "They won't let me."

"But do you want to?" the boy persisted. There was

a moment's pause; then, suddenly, his voice had lost all its confidence, he sounded almost frightened. "I thought maybe, by this time—because I . . ." With an effort he started again, and got it out: "Because I love you so much—"

My head lay hard on my arm; in my ear my own heartbeats were thick and heavy. The night—the oppressive dark—came close and warm, and those two were lost in it, held by the little light behind them for the moment only. I pressed my teeth down hard on my knuckles.

"I knew you didn't want me to say it." Steve had controlled his voice, but it was as if, for the instant, he had put all hope behind him. "But I thought it was because of the convent—you didn't want to be in love." Then he caught his breath, and was pleading with her again, however humbly. "I couldn't help thinking, if you would admit it, you loved me—a little, anyway."

"Oh, Steve! I can't be a nun, feeling like this. I know—I haven't a true vocation. It would be blasphemy." And because of her pitiful assumption of dignity, of maturity, suddenly I ceased to see Damaris as grown-up. She was pretending, pretending to be wise, to understand herself. They were too young to be out at night, without wisdom, lost in the overwhelming dark.

"But it frightens me—" Damaris choked. It was impossible not to know that she was crying. She was beyond all pretense. "—to . . . to love you—"

After that was silence. I kept my face on my arm; I smelled the grass and the earth, and insects moved close to my ear. The tenseness, the nervous quiver through the body of the boy lying there beside me told me enough. Then he nudged me, and I looked up again, peering through the leaves. Damaris had turned to Steve, her arms were on his shoulders, and he was holding her close.

She said something, drawing back a little, that I couldn't hear. Steve couldn't either, or he paid no attention. His hands on her shoulders, he spoke with a kind of boyish, breathless incredulity. "Then you do love me? Damaris, my sweet darling—Damaris—Damaris—" He repeated it, as though the name were poetry in his mind.

My heartbeats quickened, drummed in my ears. He would have to hear it now, I knew she wouldn't, couldn't—and it would be a knife in his breast. For one desperate instant my muscles were tense with the thought of leaping up, of stopping it.

"Steve—" and her voice was shaken, desperate: "I said—I can't go in the convent—but I've got to have a house built on the rock—"

"But you love me—someday—oh, not yet, I know—not for a while—but someday you will marry me?"

She put her hands on his arms and dragged them down, and backed away from him.

"I shouldn't have done that. Oh, Steve—I'm sorry. I didn't mean to let you think—I was frightened, don't you see? I didn't—I *didn't* say I love you. I don't know. But I know I can't marry you."

I had known it, too, as if from the beginning of time: that she wouldn't marry him—but never in any nightmare had I dreamed that I might have to hear her say it. If only Steve would take her word for it, and go—go away from there, quickly, quickly.

But his answer when it came voiced only his lack of comprehension. He was staying to plead with her, and it was like pleading with the water in the creek below, where it slipped over the stones with cool and low-toned voice.

"Damaris: you've got everything, I know. There's nothing I can offer you. But if you'll wait, I'll get a farm, somehow. There'd be horses to ride, anyway—you'd like that. And we wouldn't always be poor."

"I don't mean that. I'm not afraid of being poor. Anyway, Gran'pa would take care of us. It's you—"

"You don't think he would forbid it? Because my father didn't like him? Surely that's over and done with—"

"Yes, over and done with." The words were an echo, meaningless. I knew then that Damaris had never given the family quarrel a thought. But her voice was clearer and stronger; she had pulled herself together. She was going to put an end to it. I relaxed a little, ceased trembling.

She made her explanation with all the firmness there was in her. "I'm not going to marry anyone. I decided that when I was a little girl. It isn't safe. You believe in love, and trust in it, and then—it isn't there anymore."

"I'll always love you."

"How can you know? Of course you think so, but you're the most—the most uncertain boy I know. You believe in fairy tales, and you don't really *see* the people you love." She paused on that; I thought she was remembering Steve's mother. "That's all right, if they die soon enough—but I might not die." She laughed a little, with tears in her throat. "You might *see* me, someday."

"Damaris: my sweet love! I do see you—"

"And then—you do such sudden, impossible things, like burying all your money for a crazy man to dig up. Oh, Steve—don't you see how I feel about the convent? It would be forever, as long as I lived. Always the same."

"But I'll always be the same, too." He was puzzled, but stubborn. "I'm twenty-one, but if that isn't old enough we can wait. You do love me." The difficult word came more easily to his lips, now.

"In so many ways." Damaris, who a moment ago had been a frightened child, was quiet now, and gentle and patient, and far older than Steve. "The way you talk and smile, and the way you manage a horse. And all the ways you are sweet, and good—I can't tell you all the ways." She stopped for a moment, as if she were counting over to herself other items in her catalogue. "But if I married you, I'd never be at peace again. I'd be afraid all the days of my life. If I ever should marry, it wouldn't be for the things I love in you. You couldn't—ever—be the man I could marry."

This was clear enough, emphatic enough. It had cost her all her strength; she ended breathlessly. Yet when Steve would have spoken, she stopped him; she forced herself to finish.

"No—wait. That isn't all. Don't you see that I'd be the wrong person for you to marry, too? You're not sure enough, yourself, to look out for me. Both of us, we need—" and she groped desperately for a metaphor: "We need anchors. Together, we'd be driftwood."

"A farm here where I'm at home—and you, because I love you—wouldn't that be anchor enough for me?"

"Oh, Steve—don't you see? You're just dreaming

about security still, for yourself. How can you offer it to anyone else?"

If she was growing impatient with his unwillingness to accept her explanation, he was ready to let loose in bitterness the emotion he could not let himself express as grief.

"What would he be like, then—the grand man you could think of marrying?" The brief, abrupt question was edged with mockery.

She turned from him and stood gripping the rail of the bridge with both hands. "When I was a little girl, my idea of God was someone like Gran'pa, because he was so strong; when you had hold of his hand nothing could happen to you—nothing frightening. That's the kind of man I should have to marry, if I were going to marry. Someone you could give yourself up to."

"And be safe with," the taunt was wrung from him.

"Yes, someone I could love with all my heart and know that I'd be safe with, forever and ever."

There was a subdued sound of movement, a low exclamation, pleading or protest. I looked up again to see him standing behind her, his arms around her. She stepped away from the railing and from him, withdrew her hands, and put them behind her. She stood so for an instant, motionless, then turned away. As she went, she said to him over her shoulder, in the familiar tremolo voice that was hers in the presence of strangers, "His knowing that I loved him would be all he'd ever need. All I'd ever need—to be taken care of."

She walked away from him up the hill. It was a moment before he stood away from the railing and followed after her. We lay without moving until the sound of their footsteps had ceased to echo back to us in the silent air—lay there until we heard the clang of the Barkalow gate at the top of the hill. Then we rose wordlessly from our cramped positions, stretched, and hauled in the snake from the weeds across the street.

The boy who had lain beside me asked, "Weren't those your cousins, 'Liz'beth?"

"Yes," I said, fiercely. "If any one of you ever repeats a word of it, I'll never forgive you. I'll cut your throats. Cross my heart and hope to die."

And I went home alone through the dark streets and was too disconsolate even to wipe the tears from my cheeks until I stood at Grandmother's gate.

Chapter Seven

The summer had passed, almost, and in those long months since Damaris had come to Sunbury I had seen her but seldom uptown on the main street, or around the courthouse square. Now I never went on an errand that I did not meet her. Particularly, I was apt to encounter her when I went to the library, or somewhere on the way.

When I first began to run into her, I was offhand and aloof in manner. My aloofness was due to my conviction that she had broken Steve's heart, and to the excruciating embarrassment that I felt because I had inadvertently listened, and learned what I had no business knowing. After a while, I came to realize that it could not be by accident that she appeared wherever I was. I was second best—I would at least know about Steve—and she could not have feared that I would see through her. I understood all this, finally, and was moved. She had shadows under her black eyes, her mouth drooped, her lips were so soft they looked swollen. I remembered how she had thrown her arms around Steve, and wept as she confessed her love. I pitied her, and I knew that in her desolation she was more beautiful than ever.

Steve had returned to town looking ill and drawn. He said the sun had made him sick. Anyone could have believed him; his face was burned dark and stiff. The lines in his cheeks that had been so engaging that first day we saw him—the last trace of the dimples of a freckle-faced urchin—were deep and inflexible now.

Grandmother accepted his explanation and rejoiced in his idleness: it was a pity he couldn't find something to do, suitable for Barkalow blood, but he needed a rest; soon enough, if he had patience, things would work out. It was a shock to her when he told her the time had come for him to go back to the ranch.

The fates of adults lie, sometimes, at the mercy of children. It is only now, in telling it, that I ease my mind of its burden of responsibility: I remember the child sitting on the steps that morning, listening, and know that I could not have spoken.

Steve had approached Grandmother in the kitchen, as if casually, while she was preparing to wash the breakfast dishes. I waited on the steps of the summer kitchen and I heard Steve when he spoke. "Cousin Libby—you been awful good to me, but don't you reckon it's time for me to be gettin' back to Texas? They'll need me, come winter."

Grandmother was so astonished that she answered him brusquely. "Texas? What nonsense! I thought you like it here."

"Yes, I do, Cousin Libby, I like it right well. But it don't seem to like me."

"Now don't you be discouraged so easy, Steven Van Doren. You came back east to live, didn't you? You'll find something in the fall. What's the sense in goin' back to a ranch mortgaged so heavy it'll be lost the first time there's a bad season? No, Steve—don't think of it. Havin' you here is like havin' Cond back. I can't let you go."

Grandmother loved him, and she meant to be

kind. She thought he was half-sick from too hard work in the sun; she didn't guess he was being burnt and consumed by fire of another sort. I alone knew how he was in despair and wanted to run and run—for thousands of miles—and hide his face forever from Sunbury. But I couldn't tell her.

Grandmother couldn't know how he was being driven away: she would think that if he really wanted to go, he would, but if he allowed himself to be persuaded to stay, then that was what he wanted in his heart. Unless I told her, she wouldn't guess that he couldn't go—that he hadn't any money. Perhaps he had thought she would say, "If you need anything . . ." But she wouldn't: she didn't know all his money had been thrown away by Bias. And Steve would never tell her.

Nor could I. I had faithfully promised to keep it a secret. Besides, I wanted him to stay. Not for my sake, but because he belonged there, in Sunbury. I thought that by the time he had earned another hundred dollars, or Cousin Tune had come back with money to lend, perhaps by that time he would have forgotten Damaris, and would be glad that he was still in Ohio. I told myself all that, and knew it wasn't true.

After that morning I did not live, in any true sense of the word. I was waiting. For what, I could not have said, but my very breastbone knew, by the sickly hollow beneath it, that what was to come must be grief and sorrow. As a smaller child, I had dreamed sometimes of the end of the world. I felt now the same kind of apprehension as those dreams had once left with me.

Chapter Eight

After Steve had come back from the farm, he stayed close to the house and yard, and I was with him almost always. So far as I knew, he did not say again to Grandmother that he must go back to Texas. I watched him, gravely, when I thought he wasn't looking; if he managed a smile, however dubious a smile it was, the bands about my body loosened, and in a second I was hilarious, laughing and teasing, almost hysterical.

I saw Damaris only once during that time. I remember the hot afternoon, how heavy my skates were and how the air was laden with the stinging scent of dog fennel. I sat on the lowest step of the library when Damaris came hastening and almost fell over my feet.

She said, breathlessly, "Oh—wait for me, Elizabeth. I'm going out home right away."

When we had started down street, she asked me, as she always did, "How's everyone at your house?"

I was moved by sympathy. Instead of saying obtusely, indifferently, "Oh fine," I gave her his name. "We're all grand but Steve. He's back, did you know? But he worked too hard on the farm. He's talking about going home."

I turned and skated backward, a foot or two ahead of her, that I might see how she took it. She broke her step to look at me, pitifully, but she did not speak. We proceeded in silence down the shady street, Damaris walking with her habitual quick step while I skated forward and back, before and behind her. She needed to plan her next speech carefully, no doubt, that it might sound quite ordinary to me, yet would mean something to Steve if repeated to him. Finally, she caught me by the wrist as I passed close to her, and held me to her side.

"I haven't seen Steve lately. I suppose that's it: he's been out at the farm all this time."

It didn't sound so casual as it might have sounded: her voice trembled. Still, if I hadn't known, I might not have guessed.

"But then, I've been so busy. Archie Leigh's been here again. Such a nuisance." She was able to laugh, artificially. "But you know my Gran'pa. I suppose the whole town's saying he's picked Archie Leigh for a husband for me."

I was moved by sorrow for Damaris. I knew that if she had not been desperate she would never have mentioned these matters to me.

"Gran'pa's going to be fooled this time. I won't do it. I'll give up the convent if he makes me, and be a useless old maid instead of a useful one. But I'll not marry. Not anyone. Not ever." She tightened her hand on my wrists. There were tears in her eyes. "I'll always be faithful."

I saw through her ambiguity easily enough: faithful to her religion, I was to think she meant; faithful to her love, Steve would interpret it, if I told him. I thought, wickedly, "But Mr. Leigh's the kind of man you said you could marry. Like God. Anyway, he acts like he thinks so." Then I was ashamed of my wickedness, and so blurted out, "Oh, Damaris—marry Mr. Leigh and be done with it. There's no sense your being unhappy too." It was so unpremeditated a speech, and I knew so little what I intended by making it, that I was too embarrassed to look at her. I muttered, "I've got to go this way—errand for Grandmother," and skated off alone.

I did not tell Steve how Damaris had given me a message for him—and in the morning he was gone.

When he failed to come to breakfast, Grandmother took it for granted that he had gone out early. She and I went into his room to make the bed. And the bed had not been slept in.

Steve had left a note on the bureau for Grandmother. He was sorry to go this way, he had said: it would seem like he was ungrateful, and he wasn't. But if he had kept on saying he wanted to go, it would have been the same as asking for money, and he couldn't do that. She would hear from him again from Texas. In the meantime, please believe he was obliged to her for her kindness.

I remember that bedroom at that hour and time as vividly as if I had been in it yesterday. Grandmother stood stoop-shouldered at the marble-topped bureau, reflected in its tall glass, while she studied the note, first with her glasses pushed up on her forehead, and then with them over her eyes, as if, either way, she couldn't believe a word of it.

She said, "Whatever does he mean about the money? I didn't know he was in need of cash."

And so in his defense I had to tell about the gold pieces.

"That's just what he gets for being so silly." She pushed up her spectacles again to look at me. "You mean to say your Gran'pa knew about that tomfoolishness, and didn't put a stop to it? There's not a man alive that's got the gumption to come in out of the rain.

Putting money in the hands of a cracked loon like poor old Tobias—How's he going to get to Texas without any money?"

"Riding the rods." I remembered what he had said to Damaris.

"What do you mean? Stealing a ride on a freight car like a tramp? He wouldn't do that."

"He said so."

"That's what comes of working on the railroad. He'd never have thought of it otherwise. I knew no good could come of lowering himself that way. But I don't believe he'd try it, all the way to Texas. He probably knows where Tune is, and has gone to him. Tune will shake some sense into him. He'll be back. I thought he liked it here: whatever got into him, all of a sudden?"

That was the tune she harped on, all day long. "Whatever in the world possessed him?" But still I held my tongue about him and Damaris, and let Grandmother argue herself into hope: "We'll hear from him long before he reaches Texas. You mark my words."

And she was right: we did hear what happened to Steve, not that day, not the next, but the night after that. Long after we were all in bed the telephone rang, and I heard the door of the downstairs bedroom close when Gran'pa went to answer it. It rang three or four times before he reached it. But when the bell was quiet, I turned over and after a while went to sleep again, because it was a doctor's phone, and rang more nights than not. I went to sleep wondering under what skies Steve was lying, and whether—because I knew that he was fleeing from all he loved, and had nowhere in particular to go—we should ever hear from him again, whether he might not spend the rest of his life wandering, aimless and adrift.

In the morning Gran'pa was not at breakfast, and Grandmother was distraught and red-eyed: cross, grief-stricken, and remorseful, all at once. She explained to me what had to be explained: the telephone call in the night had been from a town in Illinois. Steve had been found outside the town, between the water tower and railroad track, unconscious and grievously injured: one leg was crushed and a vertebra broken. They had taken him to the hospital, and had found an address on a letter in his pocket. Whether he had fallen from a boxcar or fallen trying to get on one, or had been hit by a train, there was no one to say, and no way of knowing. Gran'pa had taken the early train to go out there and see what could be done.

"Then he isn't dead?" And I remember that, to my own horror, I laughed. But before Grandmother could say a word, I was crying, as only a child can cry, down on my knees by the dining room sofa, my arms outflung, my face buried in the striped crocheted afghan folded across its foot.

After a while Grandmother hauled me to my feet, not very gently, sat me down at the table, and poured out a cup of coffee for me.

"That's about enough out of you," she said sharply. "There's trouble enough in this house today, without having you sick on my hands. . . . No, he isn't dead."

I had repeated my question timidly while exhausted sobs shook me and the coffee cup I held in both hands.

"But if he's got a broken back, it's wicked to hope

he won't die. . . . Now, don't take on," she added more gently. "Maybe that about the broken back isn't true."

When I had washed my face, and could say "Yes" and "No" when she expected it, Grandmother began to talk to me as if I were her age, and experienced in sorrow. She had to talk, and there was no one else to listen.

"If I'd only known," she kept saying. "If I'd only known he was bent 'n' determined to go. If I'd only known he hadn't any money. He was just like Cond exactly: impulsive, then stubborn to carry out his impulses, even after there'd been time aplenty to see how silly they were." Again and again, hurt and bewildered, she exclaimed, "And I thought he liked it so well here."

I said "Yes" but I never so much as murmured "Damaris." My mind shuddered away from all thought of her.

At noon we had a telegram from Gran'pa. Steven had died without ever recovering consciousness. As soon as the inquest was over, he would bring the body home.

Grandmother was troubled by that promise, too. Should Steven be buried in Sunbury, or in Texas, with his father and mother? But Texas was a long way off: it would cost so much. . . . And she wished she knew where Tune was: it would be awful if he couldn't be found in time.

I suggested, cautiously, not sure how she would like it, "Ask Cousin John to find him for us." I knew that Cousin John Barkalow could do anything if she would only let him.

She looked at me blankly at first, then with relief. "Of course. I'm sure John would do that for me."

Cousin John telegraphed Steve's brothers, who consented to a burial in Sunbury; he found Cousin Tune and summoned him home. He sent Cousin Clara around to our house. Her first act was to pack my nightgown, comb, and toothbrush and send me over to her house to stay until the funeral was over. She didn't believe in funerals for children.

I was glad to be out of our house. But I was stunned, heartsick and defenseless, and I didn't want to see Damaris. I was afraid of what she might say, afraid of the loss of my precarious control. I need not have been so worried. Damaris was shut in her bedroom.

When she failed to come down in response to the dinner bell, her grandmother sent the maid upstairs for her. She obeyed the summons promptly, spoke to us all gravely and courteously, and took her place at the table. Beyond that she hardly troubled even to go through the motions. Food was heaped on her plate, but when she picked up her fork it clattered against the china, and she put it down again. She drank continually, little sips of her glass of water.

Cousin Clara sent me to bed after dinner; I slept early, then lay awake. Damaris was awake in the room next to me. Cousin John's walls were thick, but I could tell that she was kneeling on the stool under the picture of the Madonna that hung on the other side of the wall behind my bed. The whisper of a movement, broken breathing, a choked sob reached me, or perhaps it was merely a sense of someone close at hand, alive and in despair. I put my pillow over my ear.

On the following morning, Cousin Clara stayed at home. The funeral would be that afternoon. Damaris came to me in the library and asked me to go to Grandmother's with her. She had to go, but she couldn't go alone. She was afraid. And then she hastened to add, "Afraid of Cousin Libby. She never did like me much."

I was afraid, too—not of Grandmother—but I could not resist Damaris's pitiful eyes, her uncertain, nervous hands. I told her I would slip out the side door and meet her at the bridge over the creek; I was sure that Cousin Clara would stop me, if she knew.

When I came to the fence at the end of the yard I saw the weeping willow tree, and remembered something. I took a leaf from the tree, a broken bit of bark, and a scrap of moss from the ground at its roots, and knotted them all in my handkerchief. If I were alone with Steve for just an instant, I could tuck them down in the corner somewhere, and he wouldn't have to wait for the rain to carry him the smell of trees.

I climbed the fence and joined Damaris on the bridge. She had been watching; she said, as if she were mocking me, "Sing O, the green willow shall be my garland. . . ." Then with a sudden swift gesture she plucked up by its roots a tough plant from among the weeds beside the path. "Tansy," she said. "It's more appropriate if you're thinking of taking flowers. The country people used to fill coffins with it, so they say: it smells so strong." Then her voice broke. "Elizabeth, do you think he cared whether he got to Texas or not?"

She was asking, dreadfully, for reassurance. I gave it to her. "Yes," I said, almost furiously, "he wanted to be a poet." It seemed relevant, it proved he had something to live for.

"It could have happened, I know . . ." she said to herself, not to me. "But he was so sure of his balance. . . . Remember him, that day on the mare?"

By that time I was crying, because I didn't know myself—not really. "Oh, Damaris—he wouldn't—not that way—not purposely—"

"Oh no—oh no, I didn't mean that, I just meant—if he wasn't thinking what he was doing, he might be careless. I didn't mean to make you cry—not on the street."

She gave me her handkerchief, took me by the elbow, and hurried me along the way to Grandmother's.

Cousin Anne opened the door for us, and motioned us toward the parlor. Grandmother and Cousin Tune were there, and Uncle Aaron with two elderly cousins, and the undertaker. It was like a reception, except that the room was so hushed and quiet. From just inside the door I saw the coffin, its lid back against the wall.

I was stiffened like a stone with horror at the sight of the mask that had been Steven's face: that mask the color of tallow, with the sharp, pinched nose and the sleek hair. It was so dead. I felt—experienced—what of course I had known with my mind always: feeling rain, in a coffin—smelling tree roots, in a coffin—was a figure of speech. It meant nothing.

Damaris stood for an instant beside me in the parlor door, the tansy in her hand still. The acrid bite of its odor was not drowned by the fragrance of the lilies and carnations heaped about the coffin. Then she tossed it to one side so that the earth clinging to its roots was scattered on the carpet, she took one step and then another step into the room, cried out in anguish, under her breath, a name—and went down on her knees, on the red roses of the bright-wreathed Brussels carpet. Facing the coffin with bent head, she crossed herself, and fumbled with her hand for the crucifix at her neck.

There was an instant of shocked breathlessness. Then Grandmother went to stand beside her. The hand she laid on the girl's shoulder was gentle enough, but she spoke severely. "Control yourself, Damaris. Not here: do your praying in your own chamber. If you want to see Steven, come—get up."

Damaris was on her feet in one swift movement. Her face, like Steve's, was waxy yellow, shrunken. She looked at Grandmother, not toward the coffin, then turned and went out.

Soon only Grandmother, Cousin Tune, and I were left in the room. The two were talking together in the door, their backs toward me.

The flowers reminded me of my knotted handkerchief. There were tight bunches of asters, purple and rose, mauve and white. The sickening sweet smell of the lilies was a smothering glassed-in fragrance, not like grass and leaves and rain: it drove me to finish what I'd planned, even though now I knew the gesture was a mockery. I watched Grandmother and Cousin Tune to see that they didn't notice; I listened to what they were saying while I tried to get used enough to death to put out my hand.

Grandmother said, "Damaris has a guilty conscience, it looked to me."

Cousin Tune shrugged his shoulders. "Frightened. They're a lily-livered lot, that family." Then he turned and caught my eye. I had just got my hand back in time after tucking my bit of moss under Steve's shoulder. There was a long green stain on the silken pillow. I can imagine how I looked, breathless, shocked white and wide-eyed. Tune narrowed his eyes and stared at me.

"What is it?"

I blurted out the thing in my mind that I had meant never to tell. "They were in love with each other, but she was afraid."

He was quick of apprehension. "I told you so. Lily-livered." He crossed the room to stand beside me. For a long while he was silent, then he straightened his shoulders and said, "Well, it was long odds, and it didn't come off."

"What do you mean?" It was Grandmother. I was past caring. My only desire was to go, anywhere far enough away—but I was incapable of moving.

"I hoped when I brought him here—it was why I brought him—they would fall in love, he and Damaris. If they did, John would give the boy a start, and he mightn't have the rotten Van Doren luck all his life."

"I know. Poor Cond—" Grandmother was crying as I had often seen her cry, with tears and no sobbing, quietly. "But why, Tune? I thought you hated John Barkalow—"

Cousin Tune shrugged his shoulders. "I thought he hated us. I thought he'd forbid Damaris to have anything to do with Steve. Then, when he'd opposed them into each other's arms, he would forgive them and endow the bridegroom. But I shouldn't have gambled on it—I didn't count enough on John's good nature."

"Tune—you're blasphemous. Gambling with your own flesh and blood. Cond's boy—I hope God can forgive you. I can't." Grandmother turned and went out of the room.

Alone with Cousin Tune, I said, timidly, "I guess I'll be going now."

"Yes, you run along." All the mischief was gone

from his eye, all the jauntiness from his bearing. He moved to the window and stared out. I thought, in some surprise, "Cousin Tune's an old man."

Back at Cousin John's, I found the house in confusion. Damaris had come home in a hysterical state. She had wept for the convent: that was the refuge for which she longed. She would be a nun and have peace forever, and time enough to pray for Steve's soul and her own. Damaris was given a sedative and Gran'pa said to get her away for a while. A trip on the Great Lakes would be a good thing. In the morning, the Barkalows departed for Cleveland. I had not had a glimpse of Damaris after she had fled from Grandmother's parlor. I was never to see her again.

Chapter Nine

At Christmastime, when Mother and Father and I were in England and I felt removed from Sunbury by an infinite number of miles and aeons of time, we heard that Damaris was to marry Mr. Leigh early in the New Year. When Mother read about her in Grandmother's Christmas letter I found that after a moment's consideration, I was able to dismiss the subject entirely. Damaris Barkalow no longer had any place in my life.

I grieved for Steve when he died; I grieve for him now. But never for their own sakes do we wish the dead returned to earth. And those who die young have this blessing also: they are loved to the end, while the heart beats that loved them.

I do not quite understand why I have wanted to write of Steve and Damaris. The desire to immortalize them could not have brought me so far. I should, I suppose, like to record a world, a time, a way of life. A way of life that perhaps is no pleasanter than today's, but only seems so, and that yet, because it is forever gone, deserves a word of remembrance.

Solitary women like me, old men like Cousin Tune: in every day and time there have been many of us, clinging with all the strength of our memories to the old ways—old men and old maids who eye each other on meeting, and in that silent interchange promise to hold fast, by their futile stubbornness, in their own minds—who when they see the life they know not only doomed, but dead and very nearly forgotten, sit down alone to write the elegies.

The fields I now pass, where wheat had been harvested in June, are overgrown with weeds and grasses gone to seed. Fences are buried in goldenrod, and wild asters bloom everywhere: great clumps of purple and lavender ones mingle with the goldenrod, and in the pastures, thickly scattered, the little white ones that country people call "farewell-summer."

Because I loved Sunbury long ago, the things that have changed seem to me not to matter very much. The trees have not died: they still stand along every street. The creek still flows: beauty endures in its waters; I have seen it. There is a tall tree, a maple, whose upper branches are reflected in the shallow pool below the bridge. Along the banks there the boughs of trees are too thick for the sun to come through, except in gleams that lie for a moment, shift and are gone again. But late in the afternoon the sun shines full on the top of that maple tree, and is reflected in the water in a sheet of light.